D1552611

MY BULLY,
MY AUNT, &
HER FINAL GIFT

HAROLD PHIFER

My Bully, My Aunt, and Her Final Gift

©2024, Harold Phifer

ISBN: 979-8-35097-997-8

ISBN eBook: 979-8-35097-998-5

TABLE OF CONTENTS

Dedication to Vernon Ishkemia Phifer:

Life is almost always too short!
It's even more painful when a love one is gone too soon.
Rest in Peace dear nephew.

Love Uncle Harold

I like to thank Scout Master Allan for taking a chance on a wayward kid.
Society needs more humans like you.

In prayer, Tinderfoot Harold Phifer

AUTHOR'S INTRODUCTION

My prior novel, *Surviving Chaos: How I Found Peace at a Beach Bar*," exposed a lot of characters that affected the life of the author. Besides Mom, Aunt Kathy left a lasting imprint. She was the opposite of all things positive. At the end, it was painfully obvious she deserved a book of her very own.

Most of the contents in this story are recreated from *real-life experiences of* a lost and misguided kid. *Some things have been changed for the sake of a better read. Even though a tiny bit is pure bullshit, it's all inspired by the events lived by a* "lonely and determined little boy."

Yes, you will be shocked and amazed by the darkness and behaviors of a close blood relative. *Look at it this way:* logic and Aunt Kathy never coexisted, whereas her philosophies and *arbitrary enforcements* kept the author off-balance for much of his young life. Somehow, he *survived the chaos, abuse, and despicable treatment then* and found another way. This story definitely pulls back the covers *to* that *sick, twisted, and formative* relationship the author had to endure.

GOOD MORNING HAL

Sometimes forever isn't long enough!

It was a frosty spring morning in Kabul, Afghanistan. This was ground zero for the Taliban, yet I never felt so free. Fear for others, but peace for me. I was alone and in my own headspace. The cars, horns, stench of sewage, and Islamic morning calls to prayer beckon my attention. Well, no longer did I mind, because the rituals were my clock. The chants came day after day, same time, and same place. Meantime, people and goats made their way to fields, markets, and work. Of course, that was as normal as any other dusty day in a war-torn country.

Sad, because the animals had no voice. Life was a flip of the coin for grass, garbage, or grease. Yet, with any luck, they got to pig out with the trash instead of dinner on a skewer. Even the locals walked a fine line but to nobody's envy. They were determined and driven, with plenty of needs to go around. Their missions rarely changed. It was always constant and consistent as of yesteryear, yesterday, today, and any time going forward. Their struggles were real and imperative to survive. Food on the table wasn't a given. So, those cadences of hustle, bustle, and all other distractions were chaotic but never a bother. I really didn't mind. You see, I was still above ground and able for duty.

However, it was a different kind of day. *Old-fashioned gospels* blared from *my Apple device. Wait a minute!* Those tunes weren't my natural flavor.

But somehow, someway, spirituals were loaded into my *playlist*. It had to be an omen, *but why?* I didn't remember doing such a *thing*. Meantime, *I turned off the music and crashed into my pillow.*

Something abnormal had taken place *in my cyberspace!* Then suddenly, right on cue, the phone rang. *I let out a groan, rolled over, and reached for that cellular. Man, I couldn't reach the noise while that buzz continued. Desperately, I cleared books, pens, and a clock off the nightstand. I was willing to do anything to kill that ring.*

Finally, my I-phone found me and saved destruction to my accommodation. Unfortunately, it was the least of my problems. Someone from Butt-Fuck, Mississippi had my number, and I knew it. Maybe a beggar or scammer had broken through, which made me exposed and on the spot.

Begrudgingly, I took the call and disguised my voice. Being hacked was my assumption, so I readied myself for the challenged.

A gentleman spoke up and proclaimed he was the famous Pastor Keith of Columbus, Mississippi. If *true*, I needed to stop and give all reverence to the caller. My head was swimming! "Oh wow! Could it possibly be the guy, the man, 'The Spirit of The South?'"

"Brother Hal, how are you?" That was a familiar tone. Still, I needed to be *sure*. No one ever called me "Hal" except close boyhood friends. No way anyone else could've known that. Plus, I hadn't spoken to the pastor since I lost my mother three years ago! "Sir, I'm dealing, and things are OK." Of course, I lied. I wasn't on solid footing. I was a man without a family *living* in a war-torn country. Not only did I work in a hellhole, but Afghanistan was also my refuge. I was sustaining…but not living…life.

Still, I needed to be certain, so I threw a *curveball* to the caller just to be positive. "Sir, who are you and how did you get this number?" I didn't want to confess to someone who in fact didn't know me. Lord knows, I was deeply embedded in sin. No way I wanted such details out in the public.

"Brother, *brother* Hal, I couldn't locate any *other* members of your family, so this obligation fell on me."

That disclosure gave the stranger a unique piece of *authenticity. For sure,* my *two* brothers were as irresponsible as stray cats. Their only purpose in life were ganja, grass, and gusto.

Jerry was the oldest amongst us. He purposely took the lion share of all things good while karma graced him with the bad. Booze was his protector and enemy. Yet, he didn't give a damn to know the difference.

Tommy was the youngest and a brat on the run. First, being poor and spoiled were an oxymoron regardless how you slice it. Second, Tommy wasn't anyone to count on. His allegiance was in line with the bottle and blow more than anything else.

Sad, but nothing else mattered to my two siblings except a hit and a swallow. Even words of Mom's death came from a friend and not a family member, so the Caller indeed had tall legs to stand on.

"*Okay!* Continue Reverend." I had no choice but to listen to the news.

"Your Aunt Kathy got called home to Glory last night." For that moment, I said nothing more. *I couldn't;* I was just stunned; Aunt Kathy had *actually* moved on to another dimension! *It finally happened!* That lady *was damn near invincible! She* had survived assaults, coronaries, fevers, famines, flus, floods, plagues, pandemics, strokes, and global warming for almost 100 years. I'm willing to bet she outlived the Ice Age, but there's no way to confirm it. If anyone told the devil "You're a Lie," it was Aunt Kathy. She just had a way of coming back and back like a *sequel to a* never-ending horror story. Whenever she fell ill, she reappeared as *a new being* more hostile than the previous entity.

Aunt Kathy was the most dedicated Christian I had ever known. She would give God the glory for everything in her day-to-day existence. Yet, it was her connections to society that put my *personal* faith in troubled waters. I had never been around such a mixed bag of Christianity and evil. Because of my experiences with Aunt Kathy, I didn't know whether to fear God or fear the Devil. I was always lost and confused. However, I learned for damn sure, Aunt Kathy had to be reckoned with and should never be taken for granted! Fearing Aunt Kathy gave me *a fifty* percent chance of being right about God and *a fifty* percent chance of being wrong about the Devil. Not only did she revel in God's grace, she also frequently spoke of meeting Jesus in the afterlife. To me, Aunt Kathy was bitter to be alive and happy if she died. She accused the family of dragging her down and standing in the way of her blessings. But that wasn't all! She'd say, "I've got to be ready when the Lord calls me home" and "I got to prepare to leave here." With arrogance and contempt, Aunt Kathy frequently placed the family beneath her and her world. Heaven was just a hole punch away.

The Pastor went on to say, "I know how much your aunt meant to you and the family. She really tried to direct you guys from little grunts to young men. She was determined to make you all a pillar of Columbus and the South-side community. The congregation felt that love delivered by Sister Kathy!"

Instantly, the pendulum had swung! The Pastor was really pouring it on thick and heavy. I wished he hadn't gone that far. He was suddenly dumpster diving for something I never possessed. So immediately, I assumed it was a prank call! Or even worse, an imposter trying to punk me. Who would do such a thing? No doubt my family, Zion Gate Union Baptist, and the South-side community needed relief from Aunt Kathy's dastardly ways. But this was a cruel joke to a sordid degree! The praises *dealt* by the Pastor forced me to stop and abruptly rest my phone on the coffee table. Out of decency, I didn't want to dry heave in the ear of that Trickster. If he was indeed delivering the solemn news, his invitation should've been for a fireworks celebration on the church grounds. A spell had been lifted and joy returned to Columbus.

Yes, I was related to Aunt Kathy, but the rest of the *Reverend's* comments had to be for another parishioner. This lady *only* had love for my brother Jerry, Pastor Keith, and God. Other than God, I wouldn't know how to rank her order of affections. Aunt Kathy had no children of her own, and it showed. Throughout my life, she never showed love for any other niece, nephew, or her baby sister, which was Mom. As for friends and associates, well, they were all heathens according to my aunt. She lathered them all with pure damnations behind the scenes. So, if the stranger was *truly* the fabulous Pastor Keith, he read me the wrong script.

Fortunately, *my* mom preceded Aunt Kathy in death. I couldn't help but imagine the trauma she would've displayed had she been alive. She might have dipped into a schizophrenic rage at *the loss of* her dear sister. Aunt Kathy was *Mom's* only link to the real world. On-the-other-hand, I saw my aunt as a poor bridge to life *for anyone.* Due to Mom's condition, she would attack "The Walls" from sun-up to sun-down and day after day due to her mental paranoia. With the death of her sister, no barrier, partition, fence, or any standing surface would've been safe. That kind of trauma would've created an endless loop of rages such as: "Oh no! Oh no! Not my sister, you Devil Ass Dawg! Oh Jesus, those Dead Dawg have come and taken my sister away! Help me Jesus! Help me get those Dawg out of my house! Lawd, I can't take these Dawg howling anymore! Lawd Jesus, bring her back! Lawd, bring her back!"

Of course, I would've been the lone pigeon left to hear those tirades and shouts for days on end. Sad to say, it's *really* best Mom departed *this Earthly coil* before Aunt Kathy. Otherwise, my mother would have entered a deeper and darker vacuum unlike anything I'd ever witnessed.

After regaining conscious, I grabbed my phone and heard that peculiar guy. "Man, I missed you. I regret you never accepted a position as my Junior Minister. I need your help with the eulogy of Sister Kathy!" *With that data revealed,* the Reverend erased all doubt! He was most definitely the legendary Minister of Mississippi!

Aunt Kathy touted me as Pastor Keith, heir apparent to Zion Gate Union Baptist church. It was her way of keeping a foot in the door of heaven. She just had to cover all bases. If ever Pastor Keith got overused or jammed by the prayer line, she'd have me to stand in. Either way, somebody could testify to her holiness.

But once, I accepted the Reverend *as the real deal Pastor Keith,* a door to "The Twilight Zone" flung wide open. Even *that eerie theme music* suddenly kicked on *in my head.* Then, *right on cue,* Pastor Keith *proceeded to walk* me down memory lane while his gospels seduced my ears in the background. Yes, those spirituals were a reminder that the Minister was never far from the *word.* He was God-in-a-bottle to the *congregation* and *to* me as well. The faithful were mesmerized whenever he appeared. No, he didn't walk on water, yet I don't recall him contacting the ground. The Pastor was never seen without his long black robe. That cape extended from his shoulder to the sod of the earth from the lawn to the top of his lapel. No one ever saw his shoes, so he appeared to levitate in our presence. Without question, he was a step or two bigger than life itself.

But I'm sure he purposely used those Spiritual tunes just for me. Regardless, the music did set a tone. If that wasn't enough, the chords *playing in the distance* appeared to increase in volume whenever the Pastor went silent. Yes, I attempted to share my *consternations.* But he kept harmonizing *to his own playlist of songs and left no openings for my opinions.* I was just blocked out by his sighs and prayers being mumbled to himself. Or maybe, he was *responding to a mournful tirade from* a third party on the line. Either way, I heard only Pastor Keith. Those moments were oddly strange and kind of insulting, yet outright freakish for sure.

Still, I had to *suffer through his pontifications before advancing to details* about Aunt Kathy's memorial. He continued to deliver such prayers and incantations as, "Yes Lord" and "Guide him Father." He flooded my head before daring to answer any questions! At one point, I couldn't differentiate between his engaging me or the rhythm of his gospel. It was the most awkward conversation I've ever had with a human being. I wasn't even sure what to do in that interim.

Next, I heard him say, "Let's pray for him," in a soft yet compelling voice! "Yes Lord, let *your will* be done!" Of course, I had nothing. I was too befuddled and just decided to stay mute. Still, I waited for the Reverend to rejoin me in my feeble world. But the clock ticked on while he gave no sign of addressing my concerns. It was all about the Pastor and his Spirit consoling one another.

No doubt, my interactions with the Minister started out as weird and became more offbeat. Amazingly, I became the parrot in the store. For reasons I can't explain, "Amen" and "In Jesus' name," shot out of my mouth *in harmony* to the notes serenading my holiness! That was astounding! Somehow, I felt the urge to put on my Holy cap! *I was back among the Sanctified again...*

Just when I least expected it, the Reverend finally spoke up and came across like a Christian rapper. Every word he dropped was timed to the ebbs and flow of melody *coming through the phone.* Was it rehearsed? I wasn't sure, but he was delivering verses of his own. It was unbelievable but all in synch. The Pastor had me on a sliding board and he knew it. Still, despite *the onslaught and bombardment,* I was able to hold out *and yield* to the notion of eulogizing my aunt. I was entranced, but history had taught me well. I knew to stand firm and stay worlds away from that lifeless body.

THE COVENANT

Pastor Keith and Zion Gate Union Baptist made the members sign an agreement (1) to attend service on a regular basis or do make-ups in the terms of classes, prayer meetings, or crusades; (2) not to visit other places of worship without Pastor Keith's approval; and (3) all followers shall give or tithe every other week.

However, Aunt Kathy was just as shrewd as being wicked. First, she had Pastor Keith make a pledge to recognize her as the top servant of all parishioners. Second: after her death, Pastor Keith had to deliver her eulogy right beside her deceased body. Third: her Memorial must be held on a Monday. Since most funerals took place on the weekend, Aunt Kathy wanted top billing to other events in the city. Finally: Pastor Keith had to steer her passage toward heaven.

In return she would keep Zion Gate Union Baptist well-funded. *Oh, I didn't mention: Aunt Kathy had MONEY.*

DO ME A FAVOR

Aunt Kathy kept me involved in the church. I had to be seen carrying a Bible and touching souls. She made sure I was the Announcer, Choir boy, and Sunday school teacher. I just happened to be a menace to Columbus on my days off. But personally, I enjoyed *being a contributor to some of the wildest antics at Zion Gate Union Baptist.*

However, the pulpit gave Pastor Keith a bird's-eye view to all occurrences. For sure, I was a steady on his radar. If something happened in my region *of pews* and attention was needed, I volunteered my assistance just to get a kick out of it.

Sister Gertrude was known for disgusting potluck surprises and emotional outbursts during Pastor Keith's sermons. She was predictable on both accounts. Out of boredom, I became her duo whenever she felt moved.

Important to say, her meals were just as infamous as her Spiritual exploits. She was a loner and owner of several cats. It was widely known those animals toiled in pots, pans, and Tupperware used for meals. However, Sister Gertrude's mac-n-cheese was something to die for, yet no one warned me of the possibilities. Out of hunger and ignorance, I gobbled down a huge heaping of her specialty. Before long, furballs resurfaced and covered the rest of my Sunday's dinner. Afterwards, everyone avoided Sister Gertrude's dishes at all costs to every function. Regardless of our disdain, she kept showing up with food that went untouched.

But to keep my ruse intact, I needed Sister Gertrude more than she needed me to eat her meals. She brought excitement and attention during Sunday services. She frequently came in with tall hats, straw hats, fruit hats, and derbies with colorful feathers. We all knew the drill, but she was all mine. Once Pastor Keith hit a crescendo, Sister Gertrude would rise and jump, scream, kick, dance, and pass the hell out. Obviously, she required physical restraints to minimize damage to other parishioners and a cleanup crew for the broken pews, discarded clothing, mangled jewelry, and loose items strewn about. Yes, it took an army of ushers to physically restrain her. She was twice as big as a man. No one smaller than Shaquille O'Neal could take her down. Well, I became her parasite and First Responder. Whenever I saw a glare in her eyes, twitch in her neck, or frown on her face, I knew to move into position. But for me, getting injured was a badge of honor. I just had to be a part of her fiascos. Yet, on one Easter Sunday, I got more than I bargained for. When our youth choir created a stir, Sister Gertrude went haywire. First, she reverse dunked her grandbaby into my breadbasket. Once again, she knew I would be there for the airborne toddler. Second, a whole orchard of mixed fruits flew over my head. Third, a scarf, blouse, wig, and shoe were diverted my way. Finally, a bevy of oversized Ushers and Deacons twisted, pulled, and sacrificed themselves before Sister Gertrude went lax. It was the most outrageous display Zion Gate Union had ever seen. Mind you, she was never a disappointment for a would-be reverend like me.

On different occasions, I was allowed to move freely if I walked in step with The Word. However, other members weren't as predictable as Sister Gertrude. So, it took some scouting to help anticipate a Spiritual outburst. But when it happened, I was on the scene, *like white on rice* and waving a cardboard fan *all in the face.* For safety, I would place my hand on the back of the sanctified sister's neck to prevent headbutt to the person sitting behind them. "It's OK, It's OK! Just praise him! Go ahead and praise him," is what I would say. If someone danced in the aisles, I *joined* in and started clapping, stomping, and egging them to let it all go. Understandably, I became known as the Little Reverend. It didn't matter where I was seated, I brought the Holy Spirit to my segment of church. *Believe you me, I was on it!*

All the Elder Sisters loved me. They sought me out before being seated. They knew I was the Mini-Me to Pastor Keith. God knows, if I had been doing anything else in the House of the Lord, Aunt Kathy would have twisted me into a pretzel in front of Zion Gate Union. Not even WD-40 could've loosened that knot. However, my commitment *to good appearances* never saved my backside away from the church. Even banking on the holiness of Aunt Kathy returned nothing but late fees and overdrafts. Those beating were just a pastime. Of course, I wanted to challenge my aunt's convictions, but I knew better.

From my perspective, Aunt Kathy wanted her salvation to be *obvious,* transparent, and without question, yet my faith was always up for debate. Many times, I desperately wanted to say, "God doesn't like *ugly,*" but I was too afraid to go down that road. I didn't want my days cut short *by my vicious tirade or* from a sassy mouth.

On-the-other hand, Aunt Kathy saw my Sunday's charades as a Call to the Ministry. She even tried to encourage me with such statements as "The Lord is trying to tell you something" or "You should be in the pulpit with Pastor Keith." I resented her *prodding and* insights. Still, I took those sentiments as an opportunity to fake it all. Looking back, it was part of my rebellious nature. Without hesitation, I cashed that check every chance I got.

Still on the phone, Pastor Keith *paused his Holy Freestyling* and then reminded me of his tutelage. "You and I have been close to a Spiritual *Two-Some* on many occasions." "Yes sir, close but no cigar," I said. Without missing a beat, He unloaded with both barrels. "It was me that baptized you in the name of The Father, The Son, and The Holy Spirit." *That was true, but* I recalled, he damn near *drowned* me while attempting to rid me of my delinquent ways. "It was me who allowed you to remain in the church, when others demanded your removal." Oh man, I guess terrorizing Columbus, especially the Southside, didn't go unnoticed.

"*Son,* it was me who collected money for your college fund before you left for Mississippi State University. No one really believed in you and your future aspirations." Wow, that was harsh! But I rebounded.

"Yes Reverend," I said. "I do recall only you held things together! Sir, what else are you trying to tell me?" "Hal, *I'm glad you asked.* As a favor, I want you to come forth and praise Sister Kathy at her Memorial service."

Now, that was unexpected. I had been reluctant and coy, but he seared right through my deceptions. Surprisingly, I went speechless. Then something out of nowhere came over me, "Wow sir! I guess I'm in!" The Reverend came back with his form of excitement. "Yes, it will be the partnership we never had. It'll be a way of giving your aunt a different kind of send-off. Sister Kathy always wanted something grand and together we can be that. Just think, her favorite minister, which is me, and her beloved nephew, which is you, working in unison at her Memorial."

The pastor had done it again. He labeled me as the chosen one. Of course, I was a lot of things, but dearest of kin wasn't it. I knew then horseshit was sure to fall at that funeral.

Still suckered, I responded, "Oh man, will I get to say anything?"

"Brother Hal, you can say whatever you want."

Suddenly, I got spiritually moved. Holy Moly! Another opportunity for *Mini-Me* was laid at my feet. I couldn't believe my ears! It was finally going to happen! Quickly, I *dropped all resistance and* became one enthused idiot! If Aunt Kathy could see me now! Yep, I was rendered helpless and responded with a glorified "yes, yes, yes!" Meantime, *Pastor Keith went back to* his hymns and left me hanging all alone. Then suddenly, "Son, may God bless *you,*" and off the phone he went.

So, there I was, sitting in bed and clutching my head. The room spun round, and round, with me being the dung in the center of the toilet. What just happened? Of all people, I'd agreed to celebrate the life of Aunt Kathy!

No doubt, I became excited and stuck on stupid without thinking it all through. Aunt Kathy's Memorial was going to be The Pastor Keith and Hal show! First, *the ramifications of such a dumb* thing were slowly sinking in. I had agreed to perform at a funeral next to the Minister of Mississippi. Secondly, Pastor Keith and me would be two fools standing next to a lightning rod. God might kill the both of us for praising an assistant of the devil. Third, speaking admirations of Aunt Kathy was equal to grabbing a turd by the clean end. It was nearly impossible to say something honorable about that relative.

COME TOGETHER OVER SATAN

After 96 grueling years, Aunt Kathy's reign of terror was finally over. Her quest of destroying lives, tormenting families, and bemoaning Christians had come to an end. Satan needed her the most. That humongous development and *my agreement to her send-off* forced me to pack up and leave Afghanistan.

Meantime, I said a prayer and wrote a poem about Aunt Kathy's Last Rites. Destruction had called me back to Mississippi.

Having a job made me "The Guy" when things were in a pinch. Yet it was a dubious position. My siblings resented me for being the source when it mattered. I wasn't *involved in low-life drama*, so my brothers had no use for me. Honestly, *I had no use for them, either*. Plus, I'd been under a rock for quite some time. After losing Mom just years earlier, I didn't give a damn about a lot of things, especially relatives! My *emotional state* was jammed somewhere between paranoia, skittish*ness*, and sane. *Admittedly,* Afghanistan had been my enema to my family. Then suddenly, the death of Aunt Kathy came knocking! Well, I had a moral responsibility to prepare a grave before Satan closed the gate.

THE RABBIT HOLE

Taking bereavement leave from work wasn't a problem. But getting on a sixteen-hour flight and walking into a fog were my battles.

To lessen my struggles, the liquor onboard had to be strong and constant. Thankfully, the cabin crew gave all I needed and then some. Before long, I was back on earth in Dallas-Fort Worth International Airport with little to no memory of any details between Afghanistan and Texas. Then as planned, Deya showed up in her Buick Encore, and whisked me away to Butt-Fuck, Mississippi.

Deya had been my companion for over five years. She was a Southern blossom with deep family roots. She was five feet five inches tall with a snatch waist. Her dimples and long hair made her very easy on the eyes.

Unbeknown to her, that Louisiana background secretly intimidated my urgency to drop to a knee and produce a ring. Or maybe, I wanted to see her raise a chicken from the dead. Rumors had assured me, her tribe was capable of voodoo, spells, and such. Well, those were my on-going issues toward matrimony.

But on the other hand, Deya couldn't wait to meet the kin folks. Yes, I knew what visions of family meant to her, but sadly, I wasn't it. Still, I had to risk her involvement as a potential rope out of hell.

Meantime, we pressed onward to my dreaded hometown. I must have counted all the hog farms, catfish ponds, livestock yards, and chicken barns along our route. Being a country boy, I knew the smells, stinks, and how to identify them all. Yet dealing with my relatives and the death of Aunt Kathy were different kinds of shit to take in.

After a long, hard drive, Columbus popped up over the hill. But rather than rushing off to meet the family, I got a room to unwind and access the battles that lay ahead. But it was midday with plenty of sunshine left before nightfall. If correct, no one would expect me before the weekend. Showing up before Drink-Day-Friday or Drunk-Out-Saturday gave me an opportunity to reach people in the know. Still, the Hilton hotel was the layover needed for a recharge to my batteries. Those lavender pillows really did the job and took me down for an hour. Moments later, I was back up and ready for the journey. But for insurance, I got Deya to join me. Coming home had never been a soft spot.

Meantime, Jerry and Tommy avoided Aunt Kathy on one hand and played footsie *with her* on the other. They wanted things and financial stuff. Yes, Aunt Kathy was a challenge to be around, especially at her ripe old age. But my brothers had instabilities to add to that tango. They were always two lost shoes, or missing socks, and ill-considerate beings to fit that puzzle.

Still, Aunt Kathy played them like a fiddle. *Strange, but* they never saw her manipulative ways. At times, she pitted brother against brother, and it worked to perfection. If she promised *the two of* them a three-dollar bill, then someone had to *pull the two scrabbling hounds apart*. It was a moot point, because Jerry got first dibs anyway. *He always did.* But I'm sure Aunt Kathy jerked the brothers' chain *just* for her *own* entertainment.

She even took that scam *beyond the* grave. After her death, Jerry and Tommy discovered coins *Aunt Kathy* left specifically for them. Well, *in less than a week,* they got arrested for trading phony money. *That's just who Aunt Kathy truly was.*

No, I wasn't excited about seeing these brothers. I just wanted to *come in and have us* look like family on the day of *the* service. Sad, but I was traveling down an empty rabbit-hole unbeknown to me at the time.

Yes, the duty of finding my *two wayward* brothers fell on me. Even though I knew where to get information, those trails were likely empty and cold.

My pursuit began with Tommy. It was going to be tough because he lived the life of a nomad. After his teenage years, he left Mama's place and was never seen at the same house, hovel, hostel, shack, or bridge more than two nights in a row. He nursed the bottle and inhaled the grass. He didn't work and had never held a job. Yet, Tommy was popular at Crack houses and Booze benders. For support, he simply recreated the barter system. He borrowed and traded bicycles parts, blood, copper, chewing tobacco, screws, shoes, fish baits, car batteries, and whatever else he got his hands on. He really didn't care. He had an itch and needed money to scratch it. It was clear, *the task of locating* a bum in need of a fix was my *chore of* finding Tommy. Even though I touched a few good sources, he was invisible to those that knew him best. Sadly, my first cast went awry. So, I went on to curtain number two.

Jerry was *different;* he was the big Tuna. Even though he had a house, he was never available for anything other than a sip or swallow of liquor.

Initially, I thought of creating a city-wide hemp give-away. OK, maybe that was overkill. I just wanted to increase my odds. Time was ticking. But for shits and giggles, I decided to stop by his home anyway.

Long before my *prodigal* stop *in Old Mississippi*, my beliefs were filled with all things are possible. I truly thought I was ready for the abnormal. Mind you, I wasn't someone Jerry wanted to see. I didn't fall for his grifts nor support his vices, which rendered me inept in his eyes. Yet, getting his input and Tommy's opinion were something that needed to happen. Looking back, when Mom passed, I made all arrangements. There was no Jerry nor Tommy to add the measliest of support. Yet they were fiercely critical of everything planned, from the date of service to Mom's dressing and right down to the obituary. I thought their complaints were small, but they chose to lambast me anyway. They made no bones about their displeasures while calling me everything except a Child of God or Son of Man. At the time I didn't really give a damn. My attitude mirrored the way of the jungle; lions don't care for the opinion of sheep. Yet, I vowed to tread differently going forward. Meantime, Pastor Keith needed me, and I needed my brothers as willing participants to the big Memorial.

After taking a hot shower, I was ready for my adventure. Deya and I had dinner at the Greasy Spoon right across from the Hilton hotel. But all the heat and smoke emanating from the joint forced us to leave sooner than expected. Yet, the food was great. Next, we headed out toward Jerry's place. I had a hunch, and it was clever to follow it through.

Without a doubt, Tommy's cover was as solid as Fort Knox. With no other option, Jerry was on deck. It was time for our dreaded man to man with hopes of gathering insights to Aunt Kathy's Home-Going. The quick drive from the restaurant took longer than expected. Daylight had fallen. Previously streets of concrete and wildflowers turned into asphalt and weeds. Navigating was a bit challenging, but the stench of roadkill remained the same. So much had changed but Old Military Road was still Old Military Road. It was the anchor to a once proud, busy, Hardhat, Lunch Pail, and working-class community. But time, drugs, and lack had taken their toll. Outdated lawnmowers, vehicles without carburetors, and barking dogs without leashes were more dominant than nosy moms or weekend mechanics. So many families had just moved away. Meanwhile, residents that were left behind decorated their yards with cars on blocks and semi-trailers at the curve.

Somehow, Lady Luck smiled my way. *I really couldn't believe it:* Jerry's old jalopy was out front and parked in the grass. I made sure to pin that piece of junk in. One way or another, he was going to see me.

In the past, Jerry was rarely seen without his 70s Pontiac Wildcat being nearby. No, he wasn't about the classics. Money spent on a ride tapped into money for Gin, juice, and the Devil's lettuce.

I stepped out of Deya's car and slowly marched toward Jerry's house. I was new to the neighborhood. So, it was best I went along. For me, Jerry doing Jerry things was somewhat expected, but traumatic for others.

Meantime, a midsize Labrador mutt cut me off at the cul-de-sac. He was in desperate need of a rubdown. I gave it a thought but feared his bark and constant gruff. I locked eyes then noticed his black and white patches rotated with agitations. He yapped and yapped and bluffed mightily, but he cautiously stayed a safe distance away. Eventually, he lost all courage and quietly ran for shelter. As for me, I never stopped advancing toward my brother's place. It took some effort but I serpentine and zigzagged my way through dandelions and fast-food wrappings lying in the yard.

The closer I got, the more *definite the sounds of* dishes breaking, kids playing, infants testing their lungs, and TVs watching themselves became. Jerry and his wife had separated some time ago. Regardless, he was left with four adult daughters still in the nest. Obviously, the girls brought kids of their own to the mix. But everything unfolding before me appeared chaotic on the other side of that threshold. That entire scene grew larger and more intimidating with every timid step I took.

Right before a scrawled-up broken door were remnants of a sunscreen left hanging by a screw. The netting was torn, mostly missing, and did nothing for protection. Once again, it wasn't wise to continue but I pressed on anyway. *Arriving at the top of the steps,* I took one deep breath and delivered a rock-solid blow to the entryway.

Trust me, my banging was hard enough to shake the house. Anything less wouldn't have mattered. After several *more* jabs *to the portal,* Jerry finally appeared. He opened the door wearing an oversized wife-beater and dirty trunks to match. Funny, but he recognized me without a struggle. Immediately, I assumed he was sober, which was a good thing. Yet, seeing me wasn't expected or desired. For sure, I was the last person on his list of surprises. Jerry adjusted his head and sharpened his bloodshot eyes. It was then his booze-bated breath greeted me well before he did. Ok, he was in a stupor or maybe on the rebound. Next, soiled diapers stole the little oxygen I had left—*and I was still OUTDOORS.*

Yet somehow, I mustered enough wind to greet my brother. I tried to beat him to the punch and said, "What's up bruh?" What happened next stomped *my soul* me for years to come! He never bothered to truly acknowledge me. Yet, he responded without hesitation, "You know I can't have any company!" Then he violently *slammed the door shut!* Jerry was gone! I couldn't differentiate from being stupid or dumbstruck. I just stood silent on his porch all alone for about five minutes. I'd dealt with Jerry's nastiness many times before. But he would initially warm up before dropping his hammer. Without a doubt, l was lost, confused, and bewildered like a teen-age boy losing a prom date. Foolishly, I *used logic to* dissect my embarrassment.

First, the guy scolded me as if I should've known better! *To be fair,* Jerry was the breadwinner. His wife left him years ago. That part I understood. Only a fool would have hung around *his crazy ass. It was amazing they got together, let alone stayed that way long enough to create those children. Yet,* all his kids were pushing the ages of twenty and above. What the hell did he mean, "I can't receive any company!" Of course, *I heard those crying babies which made him a granddaddy. That was strangely obvious to his existence. Yes, the cycle continues!*

Second, I really didn't care to go inside. *I didn't want to be in his business.* I just wanted his input *on* Aunt Kathy's memorial. Clearly, he didn't care one way or another about anything I had to say. Having no choice, I turned around and briskly walked back to Deya's Encore. To my surprised, the same dog that greeted me and took refuge minutes earlier, came back to shew me away. He was craftier than before. After I got inside the car he roared, gnarled, and raised pure hell while we left that weird-ass neighborhood. Maybe his act of redemption saved his spot at Jerry's place. Obviously, I was somewhere I didn't belong!

In that moment, I felt so defeated. It was troubling to say the least. I didn't say much of anything on the drive toward the Hilton Hotel. I was in a bad way. Desperately, I needed a reversal of fortunes. Then suddenly, I knew what I needed to do. So, I stopped at the Northside cemetery. Mom was buried there. I gave Deya another pass and left her outside the gates of the cemetery. I wasn't certain but I didn't want to mix my perceived notion of Deya's Voodoo with Mom's Ghosts, Dead Dawg, and Haints. Too many demons in the same location didn't appear to be a smart thing. Once inside, I said what I needed to say, laid a rose, and headed back to retrieve my sweetheart. But I knew Deya. She had a fear of ghouls and hitchhikers hanging out in the graveyard. So wisely, I scanned her person for a Greek cross, miniature doll, or chicken foot in her possession. Fortunately, she passed my inspections. So, I left the graveyard, took the wheel, and got the hell out of that area in a haze.

After returning to our hotel, I ordered room service and devoured the remaining bottles of whiskey. Within *three* hours my younger brother, Tommy, appeared at the door to my room. *Da-yum! Word travels fast! But truth be told,* that was another shocker. I wasn't expecting him at all. Sad to say but reaching out *to my crazy kid brother* was me *just* doing what I had to do. I wasn't even sure I *wanted* to see the guy. Obviously, *Pastor Mini-Me won out.*

Tommy looked quite filthy and smelled much worst. His jeans looked overworked and dried out. His shirt wasn't good enough for a Scarecrow. Yes, my shower was available for use, but soap and water didn't appear to be his thing. Sad, but Cleanliness and Chemical dependency were never birds of a feather. On the other hand, I was bougie in his eyes. So, talks of hygiene wasn't a good place to start.

Still, I gave my plans for the funeral. "Pastor Keith and me will speak about Aunt Kathy during the Memorial service." Purposely, I failed to mention our position at her casket. "Therefore, I will not sit in the front row." Tommy nodded and gave me his approval. Next, he promised to be there.

Of course, I didn't believe him. *Why should I? This was seriously stressful, and nothing of responsibility fitted his wheel-well.* But I was listing out to sea and needed some rainbows and butterflies to fill my weary head. Tommy's stop-over gave me something good to show for my efforts.

Yet, as expected, he asked for $500 before leaving. Being bombshelled, I had to challenge him. "Why do you need so much cash?"

"Bruh, it's Zion Gate Union! You know that Collection Plate has many legs. There's the Benevolent offering, Tithes, Building fund, and money for Pastor Keith appreciation. I'm lucky to have anything for cigarettes after all that." Yikes, he had me there.

"But don't worry *Tommy,* the funeral is free."

"Well, I'm already low on gas!"

OMG! *I had to roll my eyes on that one. My money wasn't going to the church, anyway!* "Tommy, you don't need that much bread. Plus, we'll be in a limousine. It's already paid for!" "No man, I want to drive myself."

Suddenly, I got the picture. I knew Tommy didn't have a car—*I knew it and he knew that I knew it.* But he had a vice *for liquid Spice and his internal supply was* running low and *skating* on fumes. *From experience I knew once "empty," then things might turn ugly.* So, I relented and gave him what he asked for. Yes, Tommy walked away with enough Benjamins for a hotel room, *a* taxi *to and from the funeral, a generous donation to* a Booze Bender, Zion Gate Union's Building Fund, *and enough leftover change for that Crack House reunion he desperately needed.* No, it wasn't a smart thing, but *at that point* I needed a win. Still, I offered a place to stay and food to eat. Sadly, it was thanks but no thanks and out the door he went.

CHASING NUMBER 1

My big brother Jerry was the Golden child and the apple of Aunt Kathy's heart. Everyone knew this. It was vital for him to be at her Home-Going service.

Unfortunately, *neither I nor his grown-ass kids really knew* where Jerry worked. So, I *put on my Magnum, P.I. hat* and chased a few rumors and found a phone number to his jobsite.

Since I failed miserably to connect with Jerry at his home, I decided to try another route. *I punched in the digits and a pleasant female with an unmistakable Mississippi drawl answered,*

"Westpoint Construction."

Ahhhh; home!

"Please tell Jerry he has an emergency call" I said, while *adding a bit of urgency to my voice.* There was a pause, then the operator came back with, "Certainly sir."

Next, *I got a* "klik-klik!" of buttons being pushed—thank God; no canned music! Then I heard a familiar voice!

"Who is this?"

"Hey man, it's Hal!" But just like that, the phone went dead. Immediately, I called back and got the boss instead.

"Sir, will you please tell Jerry *his beloved* Aunt Kathy passed away!"

"Oh wow! *Sorry to hear that. My condolences. Yes,* of course, I will! As a matter of fact, he's right here!"

Once again, I never got a chance to speak before Jerry said, "Hey, I got to babysit tonight."

"OK! But are you going to make the funeral?"

"I don't know! I believe I'm scheduled to work that day as well!"

Just like before, the phone suddenly went *dead*! I was just stupefied by his attitude and reactions to the grave news.

Looking back, Jerry was always *kid untouchable*. It never mattered what he did. He was Aunt Kathy's baby. *In her skewed rose-colored view, Jerry could do no wrongs.* She even made sure Tommy and me only stood in *his shadows.* I mean, nothing could stain him. Aunt Kathy wouldn't allow it. She would turn his chicken-shit to chicken-salad in a snap. When Jerry got a job cleaning toilets, she reclassified it as "beautifying the company." His gig at the sanitation department got branded *to her friends* as "Out in the field." Finally, his recycling ventures were simply titled as "being on assignment." *Don't get me wrong:* I never had a problem with hard, honest, or gritty jobs, but Aunt Kathy glamorized Jerry to a fault. So, I was stumped by his lack of grief *at her passing*.

HERE WE GO!

I spent the rest of the weekend talking to Church members, relatives, and Pastor Keith. I managed to cut a deal with the Funeral Director for a change of coffins. I knew enough to know Aunt Kathy picked a bronze casket years ago. But as a speaker, I needed something made of wood for sound effects.

So, after gathering some inputs and feedbacks, I held my nose and penned Aunt Kathy's final obituary. Of course, I knew the Reverend was sure to deliver his own version. Trust me, it was wise to always stay ready.

Yep, I gave Pastor Keith my word. So, good or bad, the Memorial was set. Keeping things short and simple was my best hope. I just wanted to survive the day. Yet, I wasn't stupid. I knew the Minister of Mississippi had more details and sanctified moments bubbling below the surface.

Well, on Monday, the day of service, the skies were cloudy with constant gusts of wind. Hats had to be held down and loose items secured.

Surprisingly, Tommy showed up, but it wasn't by taxi. He walked right on site and wedged his way into the Viewing Line. It wasn' t pretty, but he was there. Tommy wore a torn polo shirt with highly visible distressed jeans. I didn't congratulate nor greet him, but I was one sibling ahead for the moment.

Next, I searched the crowds for Jerry and only Jerry. Then suddenly, he magically appeared. Of course, I was relieved, even though neither brother wanted to ride in the Limo with Deya and me. But *in contrast to frumpy*

Tommy, Jerry was perfectly outfitted—not for a funeral, but for the Seventh Street Disco Club. There was nothing suspicious about him. If maxium attention was his angle, Jerry exceeded with leaps and bounds. He wore a short pleather jacket with polyester pants. Nothing looked geniune about him. Yet, Jerry stood out like neon to nightfall. He only hid behind a pair of pink-tinted sunglasses that matched his phony trousers. Even his fingers carried the stains of cigarette burns and doobie smudges. But unlike Tommy, he donned a fresh hairdo of salt and pepper corn-rows just for the occasion. Yes, I was taken back and wasn't even sure he understood the gravity of the situation. Honestly, I really didn't care. Jerry was present and that was enough.

At the time, I was two for two, with things looking quite doable. But unfortunately, it was still early in the game. No one asked, but I knew without a doubt, booze was hidden under his wings. No, it wasn't a ritual but a must. I knew Jerry's hooch was about him and not a "Little something for the dead."

Just like Tommy, Jerry *bogarted in and* picked his own spot in the queue. Amazing how it didn't take much, because suddenly, *I let it all go.* I became indifferent and cared even less how Aunt Kathy's Last Rites turn out. That Memorial was going to be whatever it was going to be. I took a deep breath and prayed everything was short and sweet. *Never-the-less, the fact my brothers showed up, and took part in the festivities was greatly appreciated.* But those sentiments would soon change.

TEARS FROM HELL

An old African proverb says that rain on the day of your funeral are tears of the devil regretting your arrival. Well, like most horror movies, the sun disappeared, and the sky went black. *The clouds opened up and* buckets of water dropped on Columbus, Mississippi, *rinsing it from stem to stern.* Some would say, "Cats and Dogs pour out of heaven." Personally, I understood the anger of the Anti-Christ. Aunt Kathy would be Satan's problem for then to eternity. Quickly, everyone rushed inside for safety and shelter from the weather. Unbeknown to everyone, Jerry and Tommy skipped the procession toward the casket. As usual, they created their own audible of doing whatever they wanted to do.

Meantime, the grounds went wet, sloppy, mixed with mud, but a burial had to happen. Yet it was all par for the course. Aunt Kathy's life had been filled with gossip, dirt, misdeeds, and sludge. Why would I expect anything else!

During my elementary years, Aunt Kathy took Jerry and me to church services, Bible studies, and hospital visits for the sick and shut in. She had *Zion Gate Union* congregations, Deacons, and Ushers all fawning on to her. But once out of sight, she had a different characterization for each of them.

She would say *to us, with a sneer in her eye,* "Sister Alice smelled like stank on a pig, or Deacon Hunter was a huge Son-of-a-Dog, or Usher Skip

Sanders should return to the streets. He's a heathen in the church and a pothead for the corners." A lot of her rants never made sense, but she said them anyway. I never knew how to respond *when she unloaded those negativities.* So, I never said much at all. But not Jerry! He just had to mirror his favored aunt. *It was just another wedge driven between our relationships as brothers.*

Since Aunt Kathy had a car, she was drafted as chauffeur for *elderly* members to and from *Wednesday* services. Very few parishioners had vehicles, so she was an easy choice. However, accepting a ride from Aunt Kathy came at a heavy price. Passengers had to endure constant verbal assaults while *present in her car.* Even Jerry got *involved* in those character assassinations.

On one occasion, *with both Jerry and me crammed in the back seat of Aunt Kathy's Crown Victoria, along with a big basket of food, which we were forbidden to touch, Aunt Kathy set out to pick up Deacon Hunter.*

As soon as the old man settled in, Jerry wasted no time repeating what he gathered from Aunt Kathy prior to the lift. "You need to get your own car!"

Of course, Aunt Kathy *tried to laugh it off* and then replied, "Kids say the darndest things. I don't know where my baby boy got that."

Then there was the time Aunt Kathy tried to avoid Usher Skip Sanders when he came by for leftover pastries. Jerry was eight and I was five years old. Out of greed and ugliness, Aunt Kathy wanted to keep all the extra cookies from Sunday's church dinner for Jerry. Meantime, my brother and me were instructed to tell all visitors she'd stepped away for a prayer session. Jerry being the oldest couldn't wait to take the lead. Once Usher Skip Sanders showed up at the door, Jerry met him with, "Aunt Kathy said she ain't here! See, Aunt Kathy, I told him! *You can come out now!*"

Not to be forgotten in the story was Sister Alice.

My aunt drove off without her so often she had to be reminded by Pastor Keith to check on Sister Alice before services.

There were many folks on Aunt Kathy's "every week" route to and from church. In this case, there was some history, albeit minimal, to say the least between Sister Alice and Aunt Kathy. Apparently, Sister Alice said something inappropriate about Aunt Kathy's lemon cake a long time ago. Silently, I sided with Sister Alice. Anything cooked by my aunt was two thumbs down even on appearance. Like I said, I kept those thoughts to myself. But after word got back to Aunt Kathy, she "forgot" to pick up Sister Alice—even though she lived just one block over from her.

Disregarding a rider was just a ploy of Aunt Kathy's resentments. Christians deemed as soft or lukewarm to the Word got similar treatments as well. None of those parishioners were devoted enough to receive God *or a ride in Aunt Kathy's anointed Crown Vic.*

So, on a sweltering Wednesday evening in the heart of July, while heading to Bible study, Aunt Kathy stopped to pick up Sister Alice as demanded by Pastor Keith. Once Sister Alice entered the car, she greeted Jerry and me,

"Hello! You boys are two handsome young men! Y'all look like two little deacons!" Of course, I was all giggly from her comments, but Jerry returned *a compliment* without hesitation, "Your breath stinks like a pig." Immediately, I squirmed under the seat out of pure embarrassment. But Jerry stood firm and stared Sister Alice down. Aunt Kathy said not a thing while maintaining a wicked smile of approval. Sister Alice had no choice except to swallow Jerry's insult. She grabbed her chest in shock and went mute for the rest of the ride. However, she continued to accept Aunt Kathy's transportation, but she never delivered greetings to Jerry and me in the car ever again.

There was never a shortage of craziness. So, whenever around Aunt Kathy—*or anyone she talked about*—I kept my mouth closed.

I couldn't help but observe her slights and put-downs. *She showered her nastiness on everyone except the fabulous Pastor Keith. But for certain, I wasn't going to repeat any of her remarks to anyone in her presence. Of course, I knew my fate would've gone completely different.*

THE EULOGY:
UNTIL WE MEET AGAIN

Miraculously, Aunt Kathy outlasted a bevy of bogus friends, relatives, co-workers, and Christians. She had more Haters than a deck of cards has spades. Yet, they all kissed up *to my aunt* anyway. Everyone knew she was evil but played along *with their bogus Christian piety*. However, if Pastor Keith said it, Pastor Keith got it! He just happened to say, "Sister Kathy" a hell-of-a-lot.

So, the congregation was forced to tolerate my aunt until the very end. Amazing how the wicked never die and *that included my Aunt Kathy*. She outlived almost all her detractors.

Because of longevity, I was deeply curious who would attend a memorial on a Monday—for someone they all resented. To my amazement and dismay Zion Gate Union Baptist was filled to the brim. The church's capacity would normally top out at 500 spectators, yet an additional 200 got sandwiched in the pews, isles, and near the altar. Due to overflow, the building was much warmer than normal.

Like so many services before, Teddy Charles was the Usher-in-charge for placing people in their seats. He was a few years older than me and stood at six-feet-three inches tall with muscles of a teenager. He was the one guy I didn't want to see. During my early teen years, I dashed him with a pot of piss as if he made an indecent proposal. Well, on that summer night,

Teddy Charles threatened to beat my ass while standing outside my bedroom window. Once he dropped his guards, I scooped up a pint of urine from the toilet and slathered his face with little Tommy's piss. Yes, I took full advantage of being protected by Mom and the walls between Teddy Charles and me. A few weeks later, I got a smack down for the ages, but the damage was done, and history was made as me being the "Kryptonite to Bullies." But I had an inkling Teddy Charles wasn't quite over that event. The last thing I needed was another beatdown at my aunt's funeral. So, for added safety, I made sure not to display any expressions of glee. Trust me, Usher Teddy Charles did look me over but kept it professional. If there was ever a moment to pretend or reflect some grief, God knows, that was it.

My sham gave me an opportunity to span out and see the choir in full force. But looking past the altar turned to bittersweet. I saw, The Twins, Mary and Martha, singing the gospel as only they can do. Yet they were another form of bad juju for a shaken man like me. Regardless, they were as lovely as two bouquets of red roses

Still, I remembered those hidden thorns! As a kid, they delivered a double dose of whip-ass that put more knots on my head than bumps on a toad frog. Yes, I had residual wounds and a set of T-shirts from those run-ins. The wrong word or a misguided flirt could've restarted a continuum on my skull.

Mary and Martha were Boss Chicks when I entered first grade. Jerry gave me big brotherly advice on how to greet beautiful girls. His Game: "Make eye contact, give off a big smile, and then tilt your cap." Got it! I was down for a double fantasy. Well, as I approached the sisters and made the "Big Move," unfortunately they delivered a few shots and a couple of jolts respectively to my cranium that rung every bell I had. Apparently, they didn't like boys hitting on them at that stage of their youth. So, I learned to stay in my lane and never take any more tips from Jerry.

Deya and me marched in and took our spot on the front row. To no surprise, Aunt Kathy laid in style. Her coffin was a deep, dark mahogany wood with a pink-satin lining on the inside. She was dressed in a beige hat, white fur, sparkling jewelry, and gloves. Even the casket was crowned with white and purple lilies plus an 8 by 10-inch headshot of Aunt Kathy. Regardless, of the presentation, my aunt was as stiff as death itself. I couldn't remember her ever being that silent unless she was *staring you down* and waiting for your reaction to her zaniness. In my case, I gave her plenty of frozen moments because I never knew how to swallow *crazy statements,* hate, and deceit. Her *stubborn* stupidity always outweighed any reasonable logic coming from me. Even *eternally out-of-it* Jerry observed the egg on my face whenever I foolishly tried to engage her.

Sometimes, he tried to break down her logic. It was Jerry's way of educating a dummy like me.

Aunt Kathy's copy of the big King Bible drew my full curiosity. However, no one was allowed to touch it, especially me. Being six years old, an avid reader, with a thirst for knowledge, caused me to ask "Aunt Kathy, why is the big book off limits?"

"Son, your hands are unholy."

"I don't understand," I said!

Yet, before Aunt Kathy could follow up, Jerry jumped in, "Yep, you never wipe your feet or wash your paws. That's why, buddy boy!" I didn't have a clue where he got his information. Long before turning eight years old, Jerry and me practically did everything together. We even took our baths in the same tub at the same time. So, his science of reasoning was weak and idiotic at best. I was too stumped to say another word. It was useless to challenge him or my aunt.

Meantime, I was certain, there wasn't many in the audience who knew Aunt Kathy. It had to be the rumors, terrors, and past discords that brought the crowd together.

All the elderly Sisters made sure to view Aunt Kathy's body before finding their seats. Yet their observations were more than a stare. They gawked and examined her likeness for authenticity. Next, they locked eyes with one another and nodded amongst themselves. Finally, they turned my way and delivered heartfelt condolences. Elder Sister number one; "Harry, Sister Kathy was a good one! So sad, Harry, so sad!" Obviously, Sister Maggie forgot my real name. Then came elder sister number two; "You're Ms. Liza's boy, aren't you?" "Yes ma'am, Sister Pearl." Well, Ms. Liza gonna miss her sister." That was bizarre. Yet, I maintained my silence even though Mom passed away three years earlier. Last but not least was elder Sister Mable Ann; "It's going to be tough without our sister. Please tell Kerry I'm praying for him and the family." Once again, another gaffe at the funeral. Of course, she wasn't aware, but I knew she meant to say Jerry.

Still, I held my spot on the front row while waiting for my brothers. Apparently, they skipped the line just to break the seal on Jerry's concealed bottle of liquor, and then finish off a Fat One. Why would anyone waste "good weed or a fresh fifth of whiskey?" In the interim, the Reverend soothed the masses with hymns and passages of comfort. *By his words* Aunt Kathy either contributed to humanity or made the world a better place in death. *For one thing, I had my own opinion of what she did in our world. To be fair,* I was only seeing one side to that spectrum and evil was its name! But, somehow and someway, *hey,* Pastor Keith needed to show *Aunt Kathy in* a different light. *For me, he needed to earn his keep!* I was deeply entrenched in my opinions, *and for good reason.* It was going to take an exorcism or something short of a lobotomy to convince me otherwise.

Meanwhile, Jerry and Tommy got their bump up, came inside, and gave Usher Teddy Charles the slip. They chose to hang out in the foyer rather than join me and the rest of the immediate family. If spin-offs to *Mom's insane exploits were ever needed,* my brothers were perfect for casting in those roles.

Pastor Keith was standing at the head of the casket as promised in The Covenant. He garnered just as much attention as Aunt Kathy's lifeless body. Yep, he stood tall like an NBA center in a crowded market and wide like a blimp to the Super bowl.

To me, he had a creepy and divine look as he greeted the well-wishers. That face appeared to say, "Y'all came out for this? May God Bless you poor souls!"

But, as planned, *Pastor Keith's arm from his purple robe beckoned me closer. A piece of lint flew off his velvet sleeve, caught the light, and floated down into Aunt Kathy's open coffin. He stood there, fiercely smiling back at me, and demanded my assistance with a loud and forceful voice.*

"Brother Hal, come on up here. I know this is your Aunt Kathy! But I've known you longer than you've been in this world. I need you beside me. Yes, I know you are a very able young man."

There was no way around it. Pastor Keith had me on blast. Since, I *promised* to assist, he scheduled silly old me to speak as well.

On that day, *in that long-departed city*, was the moment *I was called* to find a few comforting words for *those begrimed by the loss of* Aunt Kathy. But I wasn't betting on it. Unless I was touched by the hands of God, there wouldn't be anything notable leaving my mouth.

I couldn't help but notice Usher Skip Sanders, Deacon Hunter, and Sister Alice standing at the back of the sanctuary while wearing colors only a cartoon clown would love. Their clothing had similar patterns complete with red handkerchiefs, yellow pocket squares, and green scarfs. They didn't have to utter a word. I heard them loud and clear. That wishful day had finally come. It was their chance to see the old bat off to meet her Maker.

Suddenly, Jerry stumbled toward the front but sat on the second row. That was odd because he was Aunt Kathy's next of kin. He should've been sitting in my spot. However, Zion Gate Union had grown accustomed to Jerry doing his own thang. In contrast, Tommy stayed back in the lobby because church was never for him. Obviously, he was out of sorts and needed help with his arrangement. After some negotiations, Usher Teddy Charles assured Tommy the family discount applied to him as well. Only then, he gladly accepted a seat next to the casket. OK, the people I needed the most were in the sanctuary. But for good measure, I gave my brothers a piercing look and left that circus to itself.

Regardless, Jerry and Tommy still required constant attention from the staff. Meantime, I eased my way to the closed end of the coffin. That worked out really well. No way I wanted to face my aunt while involved in that spectacle. Knowing Aunt Kathy, she conquered rigor mortis. So, it wasn't wise to lock eyes with her during the Reverend's eulogy. On the other hand, the foot-end of her coffin gave me an extra bonus. I could deliver a drum-roll for approvals and a thud for likely bullshit.

Quietly, I feared being so close to a sadistic body. I was still afraid God might reduce me to ashes for my part in that Memorial.

After standing parallel to the minister, he gave the signal to address the congregation. "Go ahead and greet our folks, Brother Hal." Without delay I spoke out. "I want to thank everyone for coming out. Aunt Kathy would be pleased by this outpouring of love and support." Out of nowhere, Jerry chimed in, "Yeah, me too! That's my aunt," he stuttered. I nodded my head. But on the inside, I knew I was center stage to his sideshow.

Right on cue, thunder rang out from the dark overcast skies. The blast caused Jerry to settle back into his seat. But Pastor Keith reclaimed the helms and preached on. The more he talked, the more comfortable I became. He read a part of Aunt Kathy's obituary a little at a time. As he spoke, I kept clearing my throat. "Ahem, Ahem!" I had seen so many preachers use that technique during my youthful days. To me, it came across as being spiritually dignified and a form of support for statements by the reverend. I seized the opportunity to use it as well. Plus, I needed another method to alert the crowd to falling horseshit and cow pies.

During the eulogy, the pastor started with siblings that preceded Aunt Kathy in death. "The first to depart was Ms. Betty. She looked strikingly like our own Sister Kathy. The only difference, one was a member of Zion Gate Union Baptist Church, and the other sister was not. We got lucky. We got the best one as far as I'm concerned!"

"Ahem! Ahem!" I wanted to challenge that assessment. Aunt Betty was very sweet and dear to the family. She was a double for my mom except she had no odd functionality. On the day of her funeral, Mom took a lapel pin right off Aunt Betty's corpse. That caused Aunt Kathy to smack my mom for all the church to see. Yes, it was weird and distasteful, but Aunt Kathy didn't shy away from making it more than it was. Not only did she hit my mom, but she also verbally undressed her while viewing the body. Yes, I would've taken Aunt Betty over Aunt Kathy on any day, year, and a million times on Sunday.

"Next; Brother Dan was the baby boy. He was just like his big sister. If she said it, Brother Dan did it. I just wished Sister Kathy made him move to Columbus and join us here at Zion Gate Union."

"Ahem! Ahem!" As I recalled, Aunt Kathy loved Uncle Dan so much, she went grocery shopping during his funeral and failed to attend his burial as well. Apparently, Ham Hocks, Collard greens, Chitlin, Fatback, and Hog-Head cheese took higher priority over his Last Rites.

Then the reverend proceeded cautiously as he introduced my mom. "Let me tell y'all about my Ms. Liza. Sister Kathy kept this one close."

"Ahem! Ahem! Ar-choo! Ahem!"

Shockingly, there was a lightening blast that rocked the building once again while dimming the lights for more than 10 seconds. The crowd turned restless, took a deep breath, and then allowed Pastor Keith to resume. "I'm gonna tell y'all, they were two kernels on a cob. When you saw Sister Kathy, you saw Sister Liza.

"Ahem! Ahem! Ahem!"

"The two of them raised those boys from seeds to bean stalks. We helped nourish them right here in Zion Gate Union. Now they're just ripe for the harvest. I hope some of you ladies can take a hint!" For a brief moment, modest laughter filled the church. Yet, it was needed because Pastor Keith had gone into uncharted waters. No one dared to challenge my mom. Yet, Pastor Keith was speaking glowingly about her. Only a few wanted to see where the Reverend was going. But most didn't care to re-open that door. Church members were so afraid of Mom, no one dared to call her by name. All parishioners would go mute and head the other way, or simply hit the exits just to avoid all encounters.

As a footnote, Mom had her derisions for society but a receptive ear for men. Honestly, that attraction flowed both ways. She had a girlish figure that caught men's attention despite her perceived psychosis. Well, that kind of concoction easily produced three bastards promptly known as Jerry, Tommy, and Hal.

But first and foremost, there was no way Aunt Kathy would appear at any venue with her sister, even as Christians. It wasn't going to happen. Yet on Sunday, they were the Superman and Clark Kent of Zion Gate Union. They never occupied the same space at the same time. Mom would sit at one end of the church and Aunt Kathy at the complete opposite.

That kind of gap between the sisters allowed me to get away with pure mayhem. Well, sometimes. Even with the chaos of the Holy Spirit, dancing in the floor, or leaping up and down, wasn't enough to shield me from Aunt Kathy. She had a radar regardless of where I sat. She had eyes liked the Bionic Woman. So, because of her interest and my fear, I was up praising the Lord long before Aunt Kathy discovered me.

Since Pastor Keith lied about Aunt Kathy and Mom, I needed to do more than clearing my throat. I damn near threw up in my mouth! Thank goodness I didn't embarrass myself with some spillage.

Next, Pastor Keith talked about survivors. He tried to reminisce and be brief at the same time. He started with Aunt Josephine.

"This was her closest sister-in-law," Pastor Keith said with a low baritone voice. "They were best buddies.

"Ahem!" I couldn't hold that one in. It was nothing but another boldface lie! Yet the pastor continued. "Sister Kathy talked of Josephine so often, I felt I knew her too." Well, they broke all ties many decades ago. Aunt Kathy never cared for women being close to her brothers. Sadly, Aunt Josephine found out the hard way. Unbeknown to her sister-in-law, Aunt Kathy penned a letter to her brother Jack, accusing Aunt Josephine of stepping out. Aunt Kathy even called Aunt Josephine a whore. My aunt supposedly used her demonic intuition as her only mode of evidence. She said, "Jack, once I saw the way your wife walked, talked, and laughed, you can bet I was able to call it. Well, little brother, she's a whore!" That was all it took for Uncle Jack to foolishly divorce his supporting wife.

As expected, Pastor Keith turned to my brothers and me. "Sister Kathy gave us Little Jerry, Tommy, and Old Hal. That's right I said it! Ms. Liza was their birth mom, but we all know those boys belong to Sister Kathy."

"Ahem, Ahem!" That guy was killing me. Now, he was laying elephant dung at the funeral! He needed taller boots and so did I.

Mom refused to allow Aunt Kathy to adopt Jerry at birth. Yet, Aunt Kathy took an unofficial role as his guardian. In the process she did everything possible to guarantee Jerry appeared superior to his siblings.

Pastor Keith kept going, "Tommy is the youngest. I don't know that young man like Little Jerry and Old Hal. Little Jerry became the mascot of Zion Gate Union or rather the 'Son of the church.' Little Jerry got to shake more hands than I did. Y'all heard of 'taking candy from a baby?' Well, that little boy took all the sweets left for me by the congregation."

Sad, but it was hard for me to watch Jerry sit and smile with a look of constipation. He was so full of it. So, once again, I was reduced to being his toilet. "There he is! There's Little Jerry sitting back in the second row. I know y'all know him! Sister Kathy brought him to us when he was just a small fish out of a pet shop. He grew up right here in Zion Gate Union. If you saw Sister Kathy, she was chasing after Little Jerry." Yes indeed, Pastor Keith got that one correct.

"I know y'all see Old Hal at the other end of this beautiful coffin. Sister Kathy promised to get him in the pulpit, but today, I've done what she couldn't do. Old Hal has always been a slippery little rascal. Give him a hand for stepping up to help me out!" Suddenly, the crowd stood to congratulate me. I had never witnessed a standing ovation at a funeral. But this wasn't a normal Memorial service either.

After the audience returned to their seats, Pastor Keith started up again. "Little Jerry and Old Hal ran this church better than I did. Little Jerry stayed in the kitchen with the food and Old Hal helped me paint, stack chairs, and clean the floors. Yes, Sister Kathy kept those boys right under her care. I have to say they had two moms. Or you can say, Sister Kathy was their mom and their daddy. She was honey when needed and a lemon when those boys got out of line."

"Ahem, Ahem!"

"Our church's sister taught all of us how to love!"

"Ahem! Ahem! Ahem!"

"Please forgive Old Hal down there. He had to fly across them oceans just to be here. It looks like he caught a cold on his way home." That was a good one, but Pastor Keith's assumption missed the mark. Yet I coyly smiled back at the reverend.

Pastor Keith picked up where he left off. His words pried open a forgotten history once he read the obituary. "Here lies a woman that would give you the shirt off her back." Yet, I knew that gift was probably laced in acid. Moments later the recipient would be fighting for their life.

"She loved her friends like family."

"Ahem! Ah-Choo! Ahem!" The clearing of my throat was followed by a loud thunderous boom. "This weather is not letting up," said Pastor Keith. On cue, the church murmurs began to swell out of concerns for the rain and lightning taking place.

Smartly, I turned away from the crowd while putting some distance between the pastor and me. A lethal bolt could've been on its way or shit could jam the fans.

Still, the reverend gave far more praises than Aunt Kathy deserved. I was faint and queasy from the tales, lies, and bullshit pies. To endure and complete the ceremony, I had to spaz out and reveal the Aunt Kathy I experienced, witnessed, and lived. Otherwise, I wasn't going to make it. If anyone knew my aunt, it was me.

HAL'S STORY: TWO OF A KIND

The shotgun house we lived in was a step up from a horse barn. It was such a despicable hovel, but it gave Mom just enough space to handle her business with "The Walls."

That place had a tin roof that leaked all the time, and a floor made of dirt and some wood. Our winters were very cold and summers sweltering hot. Even the rats took sabbaticals around those extreme seasons.

But once Mom fell into debt, Aunt Kathy took us in. Trust me, this wasn't the noble act it appeared to be. Aunt Kathy had been using Mom as a servant long before she opened her home. As a live in, she knew where Mom and me were at all times.

Aunt Kathy had a modest three-bedroom house on a half-acre lot. The place happened to be large enough for a medium-size vegetable garden. Well, the extra footage was farmed mostly by yours truly. I had to till the soil, plant the seeds, nourish and maintain the vegetation, harvest the crops, and clear the land. I worked the ground for slave wages. By that, I mean I was never paid a single dime or wooden nickel. So, Aunt Kathy's additional space wasn't appealing to me at all.

However, Mom did procrastinate and stayed longer than she should have. She burned that bridge every chance she got. To be honest, Aunt Kathy wasn't going to survive Mom, Tommy, and me. Yet, Jerry was the exception. He could have torched the place with lighter fluid and Aunt Kathy would have given him a new box of matches and a lollipop for effort.

The two sisters were never able to get along. Their biggest ordeal was Mom's battles with her demons. Mom never shied away from fights with those Dead Dawg, Ghosts, and Haints in her head. She would scream at walls and then pace to and fro until she had something vicious to level at her tormentors. It was annoying to my brothers and me, but unacceptable to Aunt Kathy. Honestly, I can't fault my aunt for tossing us out. Mom drove her to wits' end. Yet, on the other hand, moving out was a form of preserving my rear end.

Back at Mom's shotgun shack, her fights went uninterrupted. It never mattered when Jerry, Tommy, and me were out of control. She stayed on mission of whipping ghostly asses regardless of our mischievous ways. Nothing ever threw Mom off her game. Never! God knows I tried, but always to no avail. Mind you, we were three very unruly boys, but it wasn't enough to drown out Mom's rages. She just had the ability to generate a higher decibel greater than anything Jerry, Tommy, and me created combined.

Prior to our expulsion from Aunt Kathy's place, I spent my nursery and kindergarten years dreaming of my day at Mitchell Memorial elementary. Jerry was three years ahead of me. Since I did his homework, I felt deeply slighted and punished for having to wait my turn.

Aunt Kathy worked at night as an Orderly, which forced me to spend the day around her. Well, to be honest, she made me sleep all the time. She never allowed me to do anything except stay all alone in a room with no books or toys to play with. Out of pure boredom, I was overjoyed when Jerry returned home. Doing his assignments was the best part of my day. But it created a hard pill to swallow. I was more driven and knowledgeable than Jerry. So, I felt imprisoned for being too young.

Yet the upcoming year was going to be a new phase of my life. I would get to follow my big brother to the big house. I had reached that golden age of six. Finally, I was going to experience the real deal. This was no appetizer, or tater tots, or French fries. This was the whole Ore-Ida. I would be amongst the chaos like all the neighborhood kids. Everyone that knew Jerry would get to know me, too.

Since we were at Aunt Kathy's, I had to curtail my exuberance. We had nothing like the freedom at mom's shack. So, I did my best to remain out of sight. But those efforts were futile. School was just hours away. I really couldn't contain myself without medication or God forbid, a good old-fashioned ass beating.

Well, Aunt Kathy implored me to settle down. She kept issuing threat after threat with such statements, "Boy, do I need to beat the black off of you," or "Gorilla will be your name when I'm finish!" Yes, I got the message but beating my butt wasn't going to be enough. Heck, I had been waiting for three long, long years just to join Jerry. Anything short of a bullet wasn't going to stop me.

Yet those restraints were tailored for only me. Jerry happened to be just as boisterous. But he could have butchered a pig in the house and Aunt Kathy would've cheered him on. Then followed with, "That was so amazing and melodic too. My baby is a real surgeon."

Unfortunately, Mom's predicament allowed Aunt Kathy to be the greater force in our lives. All parents bought new clothes for their kids at the start of school, so Aunt Kathy tried her hand at the process. But I was too young and dumb to know the set-up. A price had to be paid for my new duds, and I was too far over the top to see the trap. It was only a matter of time before that debt came out of my hide.

Aunt Kathy got Jerry and me identical pants, socks, polos, and shoes. The only differences were our shirts. Jerry had a peppermint stripe top, and I got the wintergreen. We looked like a pair of candy-sticks out of a cigar box. Even at the age of six, I couldn't remember ever having freshly bought clothes. I was Hand-me-down Hal. Whatever Jerry didn't want, came to me. With school on the horizon and new threads to boot, man, there wasn't a chance in hell I would sleep before the big day.

Jerry normally slept at the head of the bed, and me at the foot end. The lights were off, but it didn't matter at all. I could see just enough to try on all the new clothing. I waited until Jerry fell asleep, and then laid out both outfits right beside him on the bed. It was my way of seeing what looked good on him and what gave me an edge. One minute, I was a barber-pole and the next a minty stick of chewing gum. Yet our shirts were already assigned, so it really didn't matter. I would get the top Jerry liked the least. But finally, I got undressed and jumped under the covers. Still, I kept my shoes on even in bed. I couldn't believe I had something that was never worn. I couldn't allow that high to eviscerate without smearing my entire body.

I kept projecting my introduction while Jerry snored like a lamb. He even wore a smile while he slept. Admittedly, he had a glow unlike anything I'd ever seen. It was obvious; Jerry knew things only he and Aunt Kathy were aware of! But on the next day, I would be the latest and greatest addition, known as "The Mighty Other One!"

Jerry had his normal pool of followers, and I wanted to build my own as well. Meantime, I worked on my smile and delivery.

So, when kids asked about me, I would act shy with an incriminating grin. Then playfully respond, "Who's asking?" or "How did you guess I'm related to Jerry?" But if the girls become bubbly and curious. I would add some sauce through silly replies. "You mean Jerry! Yes, I know the guy," or "He could possibly be my brother!" Afterwards, I should have them eating out of my hands. With some luck, I would gain friends just like Jerry.

When the lights came back on, I was fully dressed and ready to go. I was so neat in appearance. I had all buckles and buttons situated like ducks in a row. My patent leather shoes were laced from top to bottom with a glow to match my smile. But I was a little person and as skinny as a rail, so the tongue of my belt extended below my pockets. OK, I missed a couple of loops due to excitement, yet I was good. All the famous cowboys and crusaders carried that look, so I wanted to be just as memorable. I wanted to be popular, an action figure, or better yet, "The Mighty Other-One," Yep, Buster Brown, Urkle, or Sponge Bob Square Pants had nothing on me. Then wait, it was only five-thirty in the morning, so Aunt Kathy made me undress and take another bath.

Meantime, Jerry was still asleep. I had no idea what else to do until he and I departed for school. Class didn't start until 8 a.m. I had two-plus hours to kill. I was too thrilled to be hungry. However, breakfast at Aunt Kathy's was not a good idea. Too much of her cuisine would spoil my first day and possibly the second, third, and many days beyond.

Just as weird, was Mom initiating a fight with "The Walls." She tossed a few cuss words and hard-cutting threats and then got prepared and stepped away. She made sure to leave out before receiving a smart-ass remark from her demons. To be continued… I wasn't superstitious, yet I made sure to steer clear of that area of the house. Who knows, "The Walls" may lash out to the nearest person available.

Mom's only transportation was her infamous Schwinn-made two-wheeler. She had a thing for walking her bicycle for two blocks before getting saddled and taking off. So, I watched Mom gather her things and then dash out the door for work.

As for me, I collected all my supplies hours ago, but that train wasn't leaving until Aunt Kathy said so. Meantime, I had to endure morning rituals inside the house. Aunt Kathy would talk to herself, sing a song, and drop little prayers all around the house. Every day was just as predictable as the last. Mom was tempting the devil and Aunt Kathy would call on the Lord all before 7 a.m.

Come to find out, Aunt Kathy was intent on dropping Jerry and me off at Mitchell Memorial Elementary. Personally, I wanted to walk. I wanted to be amongst the throngs of kids that funneled toward our school. I wanted to see the cliques. I wanted to hear the conversations. I wanted everyone to see "The Mighty Other One" while being escorted by my big brother. I wanted to walk and take on all the queries. "Who are you? What's your grade? Are you Jerry's little brother?" But Aunt Kathy was stealing my moment in the sun. She just had to be seen doing something with Jerry. To my dismay, she was driving us to school.

Being mindful of Aunt Kathy's presence, I turned to reading my personal bible while sitting in the living room. It was my way of keeping my aunt at bay. Yet, my facade didn't sustain me for long. I got called to the dining table anyway. Next, I was told to follow Jerry's instructions once we left the house. Then to my surprise, Aunt Kathy prepared breakfast for me. Immediately, I was on high alert! "Oh hell, how do I get beyond this meal!"

There I was staring at bread blackened on one side and too soggy to fall off the plate. The bacon was two inches thick and fried hard enough to be a shoe insert. The grits had settled to a pace. My eggs were a perfect substitute for popcorn. Even though I had no appetite, I had to gobble something down or risk being ridiculed.

Aunt Kathy made her own homemade peach preserves. It was extremely sweet and more concentrated than Playdough. I knew if she saw me using her sauce, she'd overlook the other items I left untouched. If lucky, the fermentation was potent enough to buzz me all day long. So, I made sure she'll see me spreading that paste all over my charcoal toast. Of course, I made the yummy sound "yums" as I took bite after bite. Fortunately, Aunt Kathy fell hook, line, and sinker for my facade. "I see you love that jelly! But I'm not going to let you eat all my jam! People will pay lots of money for that good stuff!"

"Yes Ma'am," I said. Simply amazing! Being she had food she thought I liked, there was a limit. But if I hated something then I had to be force-fed.

As Aunt Kathy talked, I fumbled and moved my food around as she gave me directives for the day. "When school is over, make sure to wait on the steps for your brother."

"Yes Ma'am," I said once again.

Finally, Jerry and me were excused from breakfast. We gathered our things and got into the car while Aunt Kathy cleared the table.

Immediately, Jerry jumped in the drivers' position of the Crown Victoria while I struggled to get into the back seat. The car was huge. It had extra space under the hood and a trunk bigger than a small closet. There was room for a game of Hide-N-Seek if we needed. Still, I knew not to occupy Aunt Kathy's spot. But not Jerry, he was Aunt Kathy's co-pilot, and he knew it!

Since I was under his authority, Jerry decided to lecture me on the car operator's panel. He said, "You know D means Drive, N gets you Nothing, R is for Roll Back, and P stands for Put It Up." Jerry should have known I was intrigued with cars for quite some time and already knew all the gears. But since he was my boss, I wasn't going to correct him about his knowledge.

But he should've known, I had experience with the "Roll Back" and "Drive" features because of run-ins with Mom's boyfriends. Unfortunately, I never made it far enough for the "Put-it-up" function before getting snatched out of the car. Yes, my history of joyrides never got completely off the ground. Or, shall I say, "I never made it out of the driveway."

Meantime, it was taking Aunt Kathy far too long to clean up and take us to school. I wasn't sure about Jerry, but the anxiety was killing me. We desperately needed something else to pass the time. So, Jerry pulled out the ace, "The Car song." Just the word would send us into a frenzy. "Driver in the front let me hear your grunt. Man, in the back, show me where it's at." Jerry went "Hell Yeah, Hell Yeah!" Then it was my turn. I banged on the ceiling loud and louder with my fists and books. "Boom Boom, Boom Boom." We kept repeating "The Car song" and our simulations became even more bold and disturbing. It was, "Hell Yeah, Hell Yeah" and "Boom Boom, Boom Boom." We created more and more ruckus each time we blurted out the lyrics. It was "Hell Yeah, Hell Yeah, Hell Yeah, BOOM BOOM, BOOM BOOM, BOOM… then suddenly out of nowhere, a giant-size claw yanked me out of the car with a force unlike previous extractions. I was so discombobulated and caught mid-sentence with "BOOM BOOM" on my lips. I recalled, it was my turn to oblige Jerry with my lyrical part of "BOOM BOOM." Still under shock, I managed to absorb about six blows before I realized what in the hell was happening. Aunt Kathy was beating and taking me to the ground in one fell swoop. Even though Jerry was in Aunt Kathy's driver's seat and banging on the horn, he escaped the same shellacking I got. Afterwards, I had a hot butt for much of my first day of school. I was no way in the mood for introductions or conversations. So, I spent most of my time trying to find a comfortable spot to sit on that wasn't bruised by Aunt Kathy.

Painful to say, I was low keyed all of that day. I didn't want anyone to know I got thrashed before joining them at Mitchell Memorial. But I'm sure I fooled no one. *I had so many* dry trails of tears all over my face. Still, I stayed silent and stuck to myself in utter disappointment.

In the meantime, the classrooms were bulging with enthusiasm from the second grade upwards. All the first-year students were too new to be disobedient. They were all trying their best to look normal. But not the upper classmen. They knew the routines and were so excited to see one another. I could hear students calling Jerry even at my distant end of the hallway. Sad, but no one got to question "The Mighty Other One" because of my sour mood.

Just like years before, Jerry was quickly doing all the gopher details. He was back and forth to the principal's office with the class roster. He was cleaning erasers and sharpening pencils. Chores designated for to the teacher's pet got reassigned if Jerry was around.

Next, I got an unexpected request from the school's principal. It was quite untimely because all the students had finally settled down. Most importantly, I'd found a cool place on my little ass. Getting up for any reason, meant the process had to be restarted all over again. Mind you, Jerry warned me about prior horror stories involving the school director. This guy had been recast and promptly known as Principal Shellshock. Most of Jerry's classmates had been bruised and battered by that man. Suddenly, I was overcome with fear and with good reasons! Rumors of student transfers, police reports, and complaints were common all because of Principal Shellshock. But ironically, Jerry must have been off limits. If there was ever a kid in need of reshaping, it was Jerry. I mean, the kind of regimen where he was beaten at the top of the hour for a month. Trust me, my brother was such a rotten kid and needed that kind of adjustment.

Without further delay, I became uneasy about seeing the principal. What had I done, especially on my first day? Who would finger me for misbehaving? Did Aunt Kathy demand more punishment? I had no more room left on my little butt!

I took my time walking to the school office. I pretended to lose my way even though I knew exactly how to get to his post. Aunt Kathy had made sure of that. So, I purposely dropped by other classrooms and asked directions just to slow down the process. Suddenly, I got lucky and landed in Jerry's fourth-grade study. Once the teacher acknowledged my presence, she asked, "Hey young man, is there something I can help you with?" I pointed directly at Jerry and said, "ma'am, can I speak to that guy for a minute?" Jerry was already out of place while disrupting other kids with his miniature dump truck and G. I. Joe army tank. Even then he had toys I wasn't aware of. Obviously, he kept a batch of playthings in his locker at school. The teacher called out, "Jerry, Jerry, I think someone is here to see you!" My brother turned around with a smile and confidence to reflect his command of that room. "Yes ma'am," he said. "Oh, that's my little brother, Howard."

Damn, this nut introduced me with a name I hated. Mom had trouble with "Harold," so "Howard" came out instead. It was obvious, Aunt Kathy had given me my name. But on the positive I was quickly established as the younger sibling of Jerry. Plus, it all happened in front of upper-level classmates. Oh wow! This had to be that boost I was looking for. Those who missed me prior to the start of class, finally got to see "The Mighty Other One." Going forward, the big boys and girls will know me as the younger brother of Jerry! Finally, I had street cred over my first-grade peers.

As I stood in the door, Jerry's classmates observed our matching shirts. I couldn't help but noticed their stares that went up and down from head to toe. They couldn't believe how identical we looked in attire, yet so different in appearance. One of us was dark, me, while the other was much lighter in tone. Why would anyone dress us as twins?

Jerry finally stepped outside the room. Begrudgingly, I mentioned being called to the principal's office. Subconsciously, "Oh shit," came out of Jerry's mouth! That response said it all. It was evident I had King Kong on my heels.

Quickly, I shot back and asked if he knew anything. His response was "No." Next, I questioned if he told anyone about Aunt Kathy whipping me before school. This time he shrugged his shoulders and gave off a silly-ass smirk. I didn't find it funny at all. Then he followed up with, "You shouldn't have banged on the roof of the Crown Vic!" I couldn't believe that guy! We played "The Car Song" many times before but were never caught by Aunt

Kathy. Plus, he was much more involved with his cursing and tooting of the horn. How dare he call me out! Jerry should've been nursing a sore ass just like yours truly. Regardless, I went "ha," and left Jerry standing. Gingerly, I proceeded toward the headmaster's office.

This time I walked beyond the front door of Principal Shellshock's office. I had to do some intel just in case I was stepping in on a massacre. Well, things appeared okay from my viewpoint. But obviously, I was still green, naïve, and new to the office sacraments. I took a deep breath and went in to wait my turn for the secretary. Once inside, I noticed how starkly different the atmosphere was on the opposite side of the door. The place could've easily been mistaken for a mortuary. It was only the first day of school and kids were whimpering in fear. That image didn't bode well for me at all. There was no music or windows in this room! The only sounds came from the humming printers and pecking on the keyboards. The walls were decorated with pictures probably on loan from a psych ward. There was nothing artistic about them at all. Every display was crass, dark, and tasteless. Nothing, I mean nothing was calming or inspiring about those images.

In the meantime, I was left alone to my own solitude. As much as I tried to maintain myself, my battle had already begun. It was the silence versus the unknown. I was just churning on the inside. Occasionally, I heard screams echoing from a chamber at the back of the office. Those sounds were loud and quite disturbing. No doubt, the other degenerates besides me felt likewise!

The door stayed closed but a whole lot of cussing, chaos, and chatter oozed out of that back room. Then suddenly all conversations stopped followed by sounds of wood connecting with human flesh. The kind of noises expected at a meat locker.

Understandably, faces around me were filled with terror and shock. Students even huddled together and on top of one another. They even violated my personal space, but that didn't last long. I was smart enough to realize being near those poor souls wasn't a good look. SSo, I got up and created my excuse to hit the toilet. Well, I shouldn't have done that either. I was much too jumpy; I couldn't manage to pee straight. I missed the urinal more than a time or two. Damn, if Aunt Kathy saw my wet clothes, another beat-down was coming my way.

Still, I kept searching myself and wasn't sure of any misdeeds. Mind you, I didn't want to be mistaken or accused of something either. No, I wasn't an angel, but I was aware of all my transgressions. Last I checked, I was only down for "The Car Song." Of course, I paid dearly for that one. However, in case I overlook something or had outdated offenses, I sent up a whale of a prayer to cover all bases. Not to mention, I needed God to overlook the sham I pulled right before breakfast. I didn't actual read the Bible. However, I was only a kid and deserved a mulligan.

After returning to the office, an average-sized man passed behind me with a stride of determination. He appeared to be on a mission. Yet, no one alerted me to the dangers roaming about. They said nothing and left me ignorant to what lay ahead. Seeing that man gave me a false sense of security. "How tough can that little fellow be?" Of course, I murmured those sentiments only to myself. If that was Principal Shellshock, I didn't have much to worry about. Through my young years, I'd taken Aunt Kathy's best shots. So, to me, that man was a walk in the park. After all, he wasn't much bigger than I was. Going forward, I felt battle tested, tough, and ready to face my accuser. Once again, I was the rookie in that office. But somehow, I felt the real disciplinarian was hidden away for hard asses tougher than myself. Obviously, I was overthinking it all. That realization shattered the little confidence I manage to build. So, it was back to plans A, B, and C. But wait, there were no second or third option! No doubt, all my anxiety had fully engulfed my soul.

Next, the secretary advised me to take a seat while she notified the headmaster of my arrival. During those dreadful moments I did everything I could to remain calm. Nervously, I kept patting my foot to the floor and heard each and every tap. Suddenly, shouts of extreme havoc rung out just like the other times! "Oh God no! Jesus, please help me Lawd! I got you, Sir, I got you," were screams filling the airwaves. The door opened and a battered female raced right past me with her hands covering her face. She kept mumbling phrases that shouldn't be repeated by innocent lips. I couldn't believe those disgusting words coming out of her baby-sized mouth. Then damn, another nightmare was possibly moments away. I needed an out and fast. Fearing for my life, I formulated my plan of action. Right before Principal Shellshock steadies his paddle, I was going to blow out all the gas I reserved in my little butt. I was never a fan of the fart game, but I was scheming like a veteran. That's all I had, and it was my "A game." My intentions were to rip a good hard one that opens my belt, ruffles my pants, and sends my new shoes flying across the room. Then all options would be left to the principal. He could chance tearing into me and losing a lung or take cover and let me go. Punishing me will become a hazard to his health. For the moment, I felt really good about that notion. I didn't have much else to cling to, but I was dangerously packing breakfast from Aunt Kathy. Yes, I was sure my stink bomb defense would win that day. According to past reports, I would be the first and only kid at Mitchell Memorial to get on the scoreboard against the headmaster. Make that, Hal "1" and Principal Shell Shock "0."

Meantime, I had to go ahead and follow through before using my escape lever. The office clerk notified me, "Our director will see you now!"

Out of agitation, I became combative with the secretary. "What does he want with me," I asked.

"I'm not sure, son."

"Then why don't you ask him?"

"Hold on, young man!" She went back into the headmaster's quarters and engaged him in conversation. Suddenly, they both stepped out to address me. The principal was still holding a long piece of oak wood that was more of a weapon for war than something to discipline a child. I just couldn't believe that object he was working with! Out of fear and sassiness, I desperately wanted to ask, "What in the hell are you planning to do with that club?" **I was new to the school and was nobody's fool. But fearfully, I kept that point of view to myself.**

I couldn't help but assume I was the next victim. The principal's club had my name on it, and I knew it! Strange, how the same guy went from a dweeb to the Jolly Green Giant by simply picking up a heavy force of wood. I tried to remain calm while Principal Shellshock did all the talking. He said, "I know a relative of yours. They asked me to keep an eye on you." It was the way he supplied that information that bothered me. He had this crazed look about him. That was more than I could handle. He didn't need to say anything more. Immediately, I went into full meltdown. I couldn't believe Aunt Kathy would sic this guy on me. Didn't she get me well enough that morning! I was still simmering from her beatdown to my skin and bones. Why did she feel the need to send in The Devil-Man? I was cooked and I knew it. Just like that, I started to cry right on the spot. In the process, I spilled everything I held private. I didn't want to risk holding my apology until it was too late. So quickly, I blurted everything out, "Tell her I'm sorry! I didn't mean to bang on her car!" Little did the principal know, I was seconds from releasing a stink bomb to free myself and all remaining troublemakers. My toxic contamination would've changed Mitchell Memorial and the Southside community for years to come. "Please tell Aunt Kathy I will fix the damages when I get home! Please tell her I won't ever do it again!"

With pity and support, the principal spoke up immediately but with a soft voice. "Hold on son! Wait! It's OK! It's Ok! Who is this Aunt Kathy and what did you do?"

I went on to explain what happened before school with "The Car Song." Funny, yet he knew nothing of the incident. As he consoled me, he admitted to knowing my dad. Oh, that was the relative the principal had mentioned. I was shocked and relieved at the same time. But I didn't know of a dad. I wasn't sure if it was a good or bad omen. But the shadow of my dad saved my wary little bottom. Still, I didn't want another shepherd. Especially if he was anything like Principal Shellshock or Aunt Kathy.

The headmaster went even further. He promised to call my aunt to establish a line of communication. Sticking to his word, he tried right then and there to reach out to my Aunt Kathy. I knew she wasn't home, but I held my breath anyway. After taking Jerry and me to school, Aunt Kathy had a prayer meeting with some church members. No doubt, she would be praising Jesus in his Holy name until the sisters ran out of wine. Ring! Ring! Ring! Ring! There was no answer. Finally, I got a chance to exhale! Even though things went well with the school director, I had no confidence how a talk with

Aunt Kathy would have gone. Meanwhile, Principal Shellshock assured me, he would tell my aunt how obedient and respectful I'd been on my first day.

I nodded my head and went back to class. As far as I was concerned, I survived my initiation with the infamous Principal Shellshock. Nothing else really mattered at that point. My simmering sore ass managed to get the relief I badly needed.

Jerry and me walked home together after school. Well, it was more of me trailing him as he conversed with his friends. Meantime, I told Jerry nothing about my meeting with the principal. I knew to keep my mouth shut.

Once we got home, I went into overdrive doing my chores and staying out of sight as much as I could. Aunt Kathy said nothing about the car, so I didn't mention it either. But Jerry couldn't wait to share the details of his day. He enthusiastically talked about seeing old classmates again. He spoke about keeping the room clean. He told about his lunch. Finally, he shared how I had to see the principal. Wait! "What the hell did he say?" I nearly bit a hole in my tongue. Jerry had thrown me under the bus whether he intended to or not!

Immediately, Aunt Kathy rushed over to scold me for acting up. She was just about to cut me a "New One" when the phone rang. But she kept me close anyway by placing her fingers through my empty belt loop. If I tried to escape, she would've lost a digit or two. Yet, I stood to lose so much more than severed fingers. I was on life support, and I knew it. Out of desperation, I called on God to pull the plug! "Just make it quick!" I was running on empty once again. Then suddenly, a miracle came out of thin air. A very strange and unknown voice was on the call. It was a man with a deep, loud, and raspy tone inquiring about yours truly.

Principal Shellshock promised to affirm my good behavior on day one. Boy oh boy was I glad he rescued me with no time to spare. How ironic! Of all people, the Devil-Man would be the guy to save me from Aunt Kathy. Who would have Thunk it?

Yet the conversation kept going in a weird direction. That Caller was not the principal. Ok, then who? I overheard Aunt Kathy saying, "Hal was OK, but Jerry had a superb day." She went even deeper. "The teacher really adores Jerry. He was given duties of cleaning the chalk boards and sharpening the pencils." Some questions were asked about my preparations for school. But Aunt Kathy diverted with, "Jerry keeps the class entertained with his gadgets and conversations." Next, the man asked about my books and utensils. Aunt Kathy retorted again by saying, "I used that money to get Jerry his personal meal card. He's a finicky eater, so I made sure he had options." Last, there was a request for semester updates. Aunt Kathy yapped once more, "Jerry is really excited this year. Yes, yes, call back and I will let you know what's new with that Little Jerry boy." After that, the man became frustrated and abruptly hung up.

Mind you, I didn't care to share the spotlight of day one with anyone. I was still on edge about everything that happened from sun-up to sun-down. At first, it didn't faze me. Sure, I was barely mentioned to the Caller, but relieved nothing was said that required another thumping. Then it hit me like a wall of bricks. Aunt Kathy was very evasive to the strange man for a reason. He had to be none other than my dad. Even more disturbing, Jerry and me had different fathers, yet Aunt Kathy centered the conversations around my big brother.

Of course, I wanted to go unnoticed. But that could have been a game changer. Well, I was hoping to wear Jerry's lucky peppermint stripe shirt the following day. If it worked for him, maybe it was going to work for me on morning number two. I was so far beyond how Aunt Kathy treated me.

LETTERS TO SANTA

About four months later, I was privy to another conversation between Aunt Kathy and my dad. Sad, but it would be the last. However, it was a scam for the ages. Aunt Kathy wasted no time relaying bogus demands. "Those boys are fine. As a matter of fact, they need a new Ice Box and Sears Sewing machine for Christmas."

"Say what!"

"Yes, those rascals love my home-made ice cream. Plus, I'm the one mending their clothes." First, I never had cold treats while at Aunt Kathy's. Second, my duds consisted of iron-on patches, stiches of thread, and rows of safety pins. I was the model for Scarecrows. Just like before, my dad saw the bull and abruptly hung up the phone.

In the meantime, the holidays grew to a fever pitch. The pageantry of Christmas was much too great to ignore. Of course, no one tried to forgo it, except for me. True, I loved the magic, warmth, beauty, and good will of season, but I resented that time of the year. Facing friends with empty hands killed every Christmas wish I ever had. So, year after year, I fought a losing battle to that process. Just to survive, I followed the hype and then faked my zeal just to fit in.

Yet, those promotions were wild with nuclear overload. Everything near and far was decorated with lights, tinsels, candies, music, carols, gifts, and Christmas cards. People were revved, ready, and waiting for Santa's arrival. No human and certainly no kid resisted that grand wonderment. Obviously, I never stood a chance!

Being a rotten child somehow wasn't a thing. They all knew it was time to shape up, pray up, and wish upon a lucky star. Even the bullies scaled back their threats, shakedowns, and beatings. Christmas appealed to the goodness of heart, fantasy of kids, and the holy spirit of mankind. No doubt, it was the greatest calming mechanism and grand ordeal of a kid's life. Nothing else measured up. Nothing! Fortunately, most visions did come true. So my wishes had to matter, too.

Like (WWE) World Wrestling Entertainment, everyone contributed to those magical moments. The businesses started early for image and profits. But my oh my, they laid out sugary scenes of cakes and cookies; bright serenading lights with endless melodies; giant-size spruces, pines, firs; red and white canes; and mechanical toys with your name on it. I was spellbound and trapped in a fable.

The churches shared stories and tales of Christmas. They created plays and nativity scenes.

So I did chores, ran errands, and said my prayers, too. There had to be a Tonka truck, Hot Wheels, Rock-em-Sock-em robot, or G.I. Joe with the Kung-Fu Grip available for me as well!

Like all rituals, Zion Gate Union chipped in with skits and plays. So, I gave it my all and penned a poem. I had to reach Santa and give him my pleas, wishes, and literary charm.

A Christmas Message:

Kids,
Tis the season for cheers and jubilations
Don't worry about the weather
Forget about gripes, complaints, and frustrations
Remember your Santa's letters
Sing with your hearts
and Bow with a prayer
Talk to a neighbor

Show them that you care
Call up a friend
Reach out to a stranger
Let's come together
like shepherds to the manger
Ring all the bells
with good tidings and joy
Fill all the world
with peace and something more

Jesus was born for all of mankind
Please don't forget him
amongst the presents you may find
Merry Christmas to you
and Zion Gate Union too
Keep this spirit
with everything we do!

The End

The stage was set. I was going to win with spoken verses then add my poem and good deeds to my Wish list.

Well, The Columbus Christmas parade was soon to follow Zion Gate Union Feast of the Nativity. Suddenly, I had a chance. It was my greatest opportunity to level up and make my case. Man, I was ready and willing.

However, on my big Sunday, Aunt Kathy carried a subdued spirit. But that wasn't all. She had Peter Pan in tow, better known as Jerry. For the life of me, I didn't see the method to that madness. Yes, I was taken back, but it was kind of normal too. This time, Jerry wore a cap, vest, and even the knickerbockers of the famous Disney character. Still, it didn't matter. I had that skit all buttoned up. Once, I showed up and laid down my words, that grand prize would be all mine. Meantime, I was in the Crown Vic and on the way. In other words, I was halfway there.

Once, we arrived at Zion Gate Union Baptist Church, Mom and Jerry quickly exited the car. But Aunt Kathy instructed me to stay seated. "Oh hell," I thought! For reasons unknown, she requested a talk. Needless-to-say, I didn't have clue. I went to my corner of fear. Maybe I had another ass-whipping remaining on her Revenge Journal, so I held my breath and locked down my little butt. Aunt Kathy wasted no time and went straight for my jugular. "Jerry is reading your rhyme today."

"Excuse me," I said!

"You should be supportive of your big brother. Your time is next year," she stated.

Quickly, I frantically searched my pockets! Yep, my poem was gone. I was never a crybaby, but I teared up anyway. How could she do this? More importantly, what about Santa?

Next, Aunt Kathy forcefully told me to pull it together and then come inside. "You have much to celebrate." Finally, she got out of the Crown Vic and left me sobbing all alone. I was paralyzed and frozen solid. Once again, river tracks raced down my face. At that point, I cared less about church. Still, I knew what was good for me. I didn't want my ass broken in from the outside. So, I cleared my tears, joined the crowd, and found a seat inside Zion Gate Union. Mentally, I wanted Santa to know I did a good thing.

The congregation grew restless. The moment had come. Jerry sat front and center like an emoji. He decided to go last. After all the claps, cheers, and applauses, it was finally his turn. All parishioners roared and smiled as Peter Pan took the podium. Aunt Kathy was stoked and so full of oxygen. Then suddenly, she exhaled with a rumble far greater than all other noises made by the crowd. "That's my boy, that's my boy" reverberated crossed the room.

Jerry reached in his pocket and pulled out my stolen papers. It was awkward but he didn't care. He was arrogantly absorbing all the attention coming his way. In other words, he was just being Jerry. Unfortunately, he never read my material nor consulted with me but decided to wing it without a mere rehearsal. Jerry opened,

"A Christian Massage"

Kids,
This the season for Cheerios and Jumbo-lations.
Don't worry we-ate-there
Forget about grips…

Then Jerry went silent. Confusion engulfed the church while silence befell all mouths. "Alright, young man, alright now," escaped from Deacon Hunter! "Come on baby," and "you got this" spewed from Aunt Kathy. But Peter Pan turned to tears. It was poetic justice. Yet I couldn't take it any longer. Quickly, I bolted out of my seat and recited the verses from total recall.

"Forget about gripes, complaints, and Irritations
Remember those Santa letters
Sing with your hearts
and Bow with a prayer
Talk to a neighbor
Show them that you care
Call up a friend
Reach out to a stranger
Let's come together
Like shepherds to the manger
Ring all the bells
with good tidings and joy
Fill all the world
with peace and something more
Jesus was born for all of mankind
Please don't forget him
amongst presents you find!

Merry Christmas to you
and Zion Gate Union too
Keep this spirit
with everything we do!

The End

The church erupted and jumped to a standing ovation like a bomb in a tunnel. It was pure bedlam from door to door and wall to wall. Those bravos lasted for about five minutes non-stop. While the parishioners showered Jerry and me with whistling, praises, and accolades, I went onstage to retrieve my big brother. We walked out of that church arm-in-arms. Those cheers followed us back to Aunt Kathy's Crown Victoria.

Zion Gate Union assumed Jerry's ordeal was part of the show. My act pushed us over the top. Jerry and I took home The Spirit of Christmas grand award.

However, on the way home Aunt Kathy kept sneering at me in the rearview mirror. She didn't have to say a word. Somehow, I knew I'd crossed that proverbial line of "Stealing the Thunder" from Jerry's alias "Peter Pan." Yet, I was confused and befuddled. It was "oh wow" and "what now?" I saved Jerry from a complete melt-down in front of Zion Gate Union. That move had to amount for something. Nope, it was nothing doing! I got no respect nor appreciation. Suddenly, Aunt Kathy couldn't wait any longer. "You really pulled some slick shit today."

"Ma'am, what did I do?"

"Skippy don't sass me, boy! You didn't teach Jerry his verses!"

I swallowed deep. Heck, he stole my poem.

"By the way, who asked you to get on stage?"

My best defense was no defense. I said nothing.

"You will get yours tomorrow. Jerry and me are heading downtown. Bad little boys don't get to see Santa."

Desperately, I wanted to cry all over again, but my well was empty. Plus, she wasn't beating me. But unbeknown to her, she was way behind my game! I'd mailed dozens of letters to Old Saint Nick long before the big event at Zion Gate Union. Hell, he might stop the parade on my account. For goodness' sake, I was Santa's Pen Pal. He and I were buddies for about a month. I was just a few notes away from reaching his diamond status. But who was I fooling? I needed to see Santa. I shouldn't pass up an opportunity like that. Yes, my poem was awesome, deeds were divine and wishes too unique to ignore. Why should I leave it up to chance when Santa was going to be in my backyard. Sadly, and unfortunately, Mom never said a word during my tongue lashing. She sat silent and stared in the distance. Of course, I knew she didn't have the weight to provide any relief anyway.

Meantime, I had Aunt Kathy and Mom routines down to a science. I knew their schemes for, breakfast, lunch, dinner, bed, and minutes in showers. I didn't have to see them to know who was doing what. So, when Jerry was asleep or not around, I could sneak out of the house and return undetected with ease. Contrary to punishment, I was going to the Columbus Christmas Parade out of protest and personal desire.

For good measure, I knew Aunt Kathy's pattern of visiting church members after big events. By calculations, I had plenty of time to leave and return without cause for concerns.

The day of the big parade came in like a whirlwind. It was Monday and I had a date with Santa. It was early December, and the temperatures were far warmer than normal. That was incredible for me. Since, I didn't have much of a coat, Mother Nature really looked out.

I went through my chores as planned then pulled out every schoolbook I had. I knew math very well, but I wrote down the entire multiplication chart just to appear occupied.

Once Aunt Kathy and Jerry walked out the door, I started my count-down. Of course, Mom was home but was keenly focused on "The Walls!" To be sure, I peaked in and saw Mom pacing the floor and talking shit before battle. "I wish you would! Yeah, fuck around and find out! Your ass belongs to me!" Yep, I was good. Living with Aunt Kathy had been a strain on the war. It was hard for Mom to gain any leverage at her sister's place. But on Monday night, it was "Game On" and time to "Take No Prisoners."

For insurance, I took note of everything Aunt Kathy and Jerry had on. Lord knows, I didn't need any surprises while out on the streets. I didn't need a slip-up of any form. Otherwise, I'd be basting on a skewer complete with a rutabaga jammed down my throat.

My plan appeared on target. But I had to wait for the "First Lick." One Mississippi, two Mississippi, three Mississippi, shit was about to go down. Those Haints, Devils, and Ghosts had it coming. Then it happened. "You Devil-Ass Dawgs!" That was it! Mom had zoned out. That fight was on, and it was "Good Night Irene." It didn't matter if I slammed the door, broke a window, or shot a gun. It was all to the good now.

Getting to the parade was as simple as walking due north. I had been downtown far too many times to get lost. Plus, my journey was made easier because all revelers were heading my way.

Before I saw the motorcades, I felt the jingles in the air. I was so over-joyed to be amongst the madnesses. I could hear the bands and the bull horns blaring out the details. There was music behind me, songs beside me, and melodies carrying me forward. The Carolers started up, and then repeated in rotation after rotation. I was getting closer, but still no "Ho Ho Ho."

Finally, I made it to the heart of the show. This was my first Christmas parade, and it was right out of a dream. There were dancers, clowns, soldiers, bands, firemen, policemen, the Rotary, the Jaycees, the Kiwanis, the Amer-ican Legion, the VFW, the AMVETS, Boy Scouts, Girl Scouts, Cub Scouts, Brownies, and 4-H clubs, just to name a few. There were funny cars, tractors, trucks, and motorcycles weaving throughout the streets. Amazing, but there were horses and ponies for days upon days. I knew then I wanted to join a Kid's club. Someway and somehow, I had to become a part of that revelry!

On-the-other hand, it was hard to ignore the kiosks with popcorn, hotdogs, coco, turkey legs, and funnel cakes for sale. The food found me before I discovered it. That aroma practically stopped me in my tracks. Those smells reminded me of an empty stomach. Initially, I couldn't eat. I was far too excited and determined to see Santa. I lost my appetite in the haste. But all the traveling and moving about suddenly made me hungry. None-the-less, I didn't have any money. So, snacks became just another big distraction. Still, there were tons of peppermint sticks, cookies, and chocolate bells being tossed about the parade route. So, I grabbed what others had missed or over-looked and ate what I could.

Still, there were people, events, and food galore, but no sign of Santa.

Yet, the parade marched on. I saw dancing elves, smiling angels, camels, goats, sheep, but not a gray beard amongst them.

As time ticked on, my fear crept in. So, I had to stop just to evaluate my fate. If caught, I'd get a mudhole stumped out of my ass for damn sure. But I had to stand on my square. This was my mission and my reward. For once, forget about my butt and skinny bones. Nothing had ever captivated like the

Columbus parade. Retreat wasn't an option. All things near and far were all about Christmas. It was the merriment of a lifetime. Yes, Aunt Kathy would maul and hurt me badly, but the scars would heal. Then suddenly, something cryptic came over me. Aunt Kathy wasn't leaving that parade until Jerry saw Santa Claus. By default, my big brother got me more time and optimism.

Somewhere among all the confusion were Aunt Kathy and Jerry roaming like predators on the Serengeti. But, so far so good, my cover was still intact. So carefully, I pushed onward.

An hour later, the kids became restless and started to rush Main Street. The workers went into overdrive. Children were crossing the yellow lines and blocking the floats. Unfortunately, I was new and fell farther behind the others. Like magic, it suddenly happened. Electricity filled the air! Eyes were bulging and mouths were screaming! Everyone knew something big was happening—except me! Yes, I couldn't see a thing! Not even one i-o-ta of sight came my way. Yes, I felt the presence, but that was all. "Ho Ho Ho," he said! It was Santa! It was Old Saint Nick! But I was stuck in the back of the crowd. I could hear him, and I heard him clearly, but that was all! Quickly, I climbed the nearest lamp post. Like an illusion, there he was! A Big Jolly guy with a bulging midsection! He was gleefully waving back and forth to all the kids! He was showering the mob with candy, Ho Ho's, and a whole lot more!

Immediately, I started to panic. I needed to reach that float. I had to give Santa my letters. I wanted to get eye to eye. Yes, he was merry and happy, yet he was searching for little old me. Dammit, somebody had to let me through. But those kids weren't stupid. They had letters and Christmas wishes, too.

Next, I ran fast and farther ahead of the motorcade. All the kids had jammed the routes and left huge gaps out front of the sleigh. After finding my opening, I got inside where Santa would next likely appear! It was exhausting but I made it! I saw the giant sleigh and screamed at the top of my lungs, "Santa, Santa," and "Santa!" Finally, I flashed my letters and yelled louder than ever before. Yet, it was all a blur. My advantage was only short-lived. I got swallowed up by a crazed bunch of youngsters. I was just a crumb to a bed of ants. All the pushing and shoving sent me reeling to the pavement. In the process, I lost all my information. When I recovered, a thousand elves and small human-beings stood above, around, and next to me. Yes, I regained my footing but not my letters. Frantically, I searched and searched, but to no avail. My work, kudos, and dreams had drifted into the night like the streamers, tinsels, and confetti filling the cool Mississippi air. Yet, being angry and dismayed didn't stop the Big Red Sleigh from moving away. Suddenly, all my emptiness came rushing forward. It was my first Columbus parade, and I let Santa down. But he wasn't alone, I disappointed myself as well.

Sadly, I had no choice other than return home. I was so dejected and broken. I started kicking paper cups, glow sticks, and stale caramel-corn lying on the sidewalks. I had a long and painful journey ahead of me. Then, out of nowhere, I saw a familiar little fellow walking step for step and cadence to cadence, but on the other side of the street. Obviously, he fared much better than I did. He was holding a stuffed Unicorn while choking down a twelve-inch frankfurter. His shirt received the buck of the condiments. All the mustard and mayo provided great cover, yet I knew that kid well because it was JERRY! Then suddenly, it was SHIT! DAMN, DAMN, and OH DAMN! He was wearing the green peppermint polo, whereas I purposely picked out the red striped to line up with Santa. Yes, he had chocolate, grease, and cotton candy stains all over him, yet why did it take so long to identify my brother? OK, he could've passed for a yellow and beige Minion, but that was a poor excuse on my part. Mind you, the parade could've used him as an Extra. But if that was Jerry, then where in the hell was AUNT KATHY?

Quickly, I started my dash back to the Southside like a fugitive stalked by bloodhounds. I couldn't believe I damn near walked into the Lion's Den! Only a fool would wait around. Immediately, I tried to blend with the masses. So, I walked close to other families trekking to my side of town. My heart skipped-a-beat with every passing car. I was completely paranoid and rightfully so. In my head Aunt Kathy drove every vehicle that came my way. Mind you, leaving me behind was meant as punishment. If she knew I was out on my own, then I'd better get out of Columbus and fast. Creating a new underground railroad wasn't a bad idea! I mean, leave the city right away. One minute of hesitation was the difference between having an ass and being left with half-a-loaf to sit on! Desperately, I tried to hurry my pace, but the crowd was much too thick. The noises were loud, but that was expected. However, getting beyond them was my dilemma.

As I traveled, I went through entire middle-class communities completely occupied by white residents, yet they understood. Thongs of kids flooded the yards and poured into street, and it was all good. After all, it was Christmas. These neighbors were well aware of little grunts serenading and snaking their way home on a parade high. If that wasn't enough, family after family kept caroling and holding hands, but stayed in my damn way. All that residual joy and celebration had me sandwiched between a bad spot and a visit to the emergency room.

Regardless, I needed to get home and in a haze! Time was crucial. I had to return or forget about ever seeing another Christmas. Still, those youngsters kept singing, prancing, and impeding my way. Needless-to-say, they stood between life and death! But I was out of options. So, I threw down my Christian-Card like never before. I pleaded with God to keep me out of the hands of Satan.

Yes, I made a hard bed and couldn't accept my fate. But I had to see Santa. Yet, unfortunately, it was time to face the music.

I prayed and prayed until I entered the driveway. Only then, I changed to "Thank you, God" and "Holy Jesus, Hallelujah," I've finally made it! There was no Crown Vic resting in the garage. I let out a huge sigh of relief and cleared the water off my weary head. It was nothing but the grace of God that carried me home. No vehicle meant no Aunt Kathy or Jerry. Man, I'd survived to see another day.

Softly, I turned the doorknob and walked inside. The house was slightly dimmed. Nothing had changed from the way I left. Honestly, Aunt Kathy did have the jump and should've beaten me to the house with minutes to spare. Yet, she veered off to visit a church member as predicted. Weird, but Christians love to praise Jesus in the wee hours of the morning. Well, her convictions saved little old me in a mysterious way.

I creeped through the house and heard Mom's rants draining to a trickle. Just to be sure, I sneaked-a-peak at her. She was sweating profusely but still in one piece. I didn't see any carnage, plus I was back on the inside.

That's all that mattered. Still, I was tired and panting like an overworked mule. Yet, I was too scared to think about food. So, I jumped into bed to complete my cover. I knew Aunt Kathy's and Jerry's return were moments away.

Just as expected, the Crown Vic pulled into its usual spot. The car doors came open and Jerry quickly bounced out with a Christmas buzz. He was still drunk with excitement. With spirit and joy, he belted out his version of a holiday melody. "*Dashing through the STORE, on A one horse Open Day, through the BELLS we go, laughing all the way, ha ha ha !*"

"Shish Shish, don't wake up the neighbors," said Aunt Kathy.

Finally, the two of them meandered inside. Aunt Kathy went one way, and Jerry stepped into the bedroom. Strange, but that stuffed Unicorn never made its appearance at my aunt's house.

EASTER HERE, EASTER THERE

Even though Christmas was the granddaddy of holidays, Resurrection Sunday stood tall as well. Easter was all about sacrifice and renewal. But I wasn't aware of anyone reframing from anything, yet everyone had something to show. Kids got brand new clothing, gift baskets, flowers, and bonnets. This was Spring. It was an opportunity to exploit the cuteness of the little ones under the rebirth of a new season.

Of course, Zion Gate Union helped build that platform. They created Egg Hunts, Readings, Recitals, and Revivals. Jerry was always a participant, but Tommy and me changed the game. Aunt Kathy never passed up a chance to put Jerry on display. His age didn't matter. He was twelve and needed to step aside, yet Aunt Kathy wouldn't allow it.

Looking back, I was nine years old, and Tommy was three. Jerry would get a suit just for this occasion. Easter was heavy on appearance and low on performance. Therefore, Tommy and me never really bothered to get involved. Our roles were background support, particularly for Jerry.

Zion Gate Union used the contests as money makers for the church.

To enter the Big Egg Hunt, each kid had to have a registered basket and a donation from a financial backer. Whoever discovered the most eggs was the victor. In the end, the winner got to keep their cluster, plus a book of coupons for free treats from Fast-Food vendors around town. However, an opportunity for outside snacks was all it took for Jerry, Tommy, and me to team up. Our craving for junk was real. With goodies on the line, we upped the ante.

Well, neither Mom nor Aunt Kathy was sponsoring Tommy and me. So, Jerry became an automatic shoe-in. Mind up, Mom wasn't going to contribute to anything unless she was selling Jerry's multitude back to the church.

Meantime, I created my own scheme for the process. On the night of Holy Saturday, I dyed a few eggs to mimic the originals. Throw in a couple of golf balls and my plan of distraction was on point. All I had to do was plant the counterfeits right before The Big Hunt, and then make sure Jerry knew where the fakes were. That move gave the brothers and me a huge advantage.

On the morning of Easter, all the kids marveled at the new hats, suits, shoes, and baskets delivered by the Magic Bunny. Even the parents carried a glow as bright as the children. They were proud and overjoyed to see those small buds blossom into little misses and juniors.

The Big Hunt always kicked-off right after Sunday school.

My plan was set. Tommy and me would direct Jerry to all places of suspected hidden treasures. But wait, that wasn't all, we had a secret agent. Aunt Kathy was part of the staff in charge of Children' Activities. She coordinated the Egg Hunt! Yet, she never got Tommy and me the Hook-Up. But once the event got underway, Aunt Kathy did her best to point Jerry toward concealed eggs. Yes, Tommy and me were thankful for the inside help, but Jerry was already in our pockets. Mind you, if Aunt Kathy knew the real scam, she would have tanned the hides off Tommy and me. Strange, it was OK for her to cheat but sinful for us to do so.

Fast-Food was a rarity, so winning the Big Hunt was a major accomplishment. Plus, it gave us some relief from Aunt Kathy's mystery meals.

Weird, but even with Aunt Kathy's support, Jerry was unable to bring home the grand prize. He lost a couple of years back-to-back and then realized he needed his brother's involvement.

Before the tournament got under way, Tommy and me would find a buried nest and then drop a decoy just to confuse or slow down the competition. When the final tally came in, Jerry would win or place in the top tier. Even with the fix, Jerry still had counterfeits amongst his stashes. Yet, he wasn't alone in quirkiness. For reasons unknown, Mom collected all the empty baskets discarded by the losers just for her own keepsake.

Next, we returned for Resurrection Sunday later in the evening. That service consisted of plays, speeches, songs, and sermons.

Adults would go first. Next, the choir would follow with songs about Old Calvary and how Jesus died for mankind. Those hymns created a spirit hotter than a fever inside Zion Gate Union. Christians were visibly touched by the reenactment of Jesus' march to crucifixion. They shouted, "Look what they did, Lawd, look what they did! Nobody stood with you. But I'm here, Lawd, I'm here!" Aunt Kathy never took a backseat to anyone, "Just Evil, Lawd! Just Evil!" It was the kettle pointing at the pot or the pot criticizing the kettle. Either way, it was irony at its purest form.

Finally, kids took the floor. The parents were just as nervous as the little ones. I had nothing fresh, so I went first just to get it over with. Still, I delivered without errors. Next, the kindergartners followed and allowed Little Tommy to deliver his poem,

Easter, I shall shout
Easter is what Jesus is about.

He was flawless. Little Tommy immediately received a big round of applause. After that, Jerry couldn't wait any longer. Initially, he stepped aside when the pre-teens took the floor. Instead of waiting his turn, he wanted the love Little Tommy received. So, Jerry jumped in and addressed the crowd before his scheduled slot. Well, that wasn't part of the plan. He really needed a walk-through but decided to go ahead on his own. Suddenly, it was "Go Time."

Jerry's initial verse:

Flowers have bloomed
Chirping in the air
A new beginning
Cause Easter is here.

But Jerry was a Wild Card. He forged ahead with twinkle and cheese from ear to ear and jawline to jawline.

Flowers, Bloom, Easter
Chirp Chirp Air

Jerry had blown it. The crowd held firm as Jerry attempted a redo.

Flowers Chirp,
Bloom Easter.

This time, parishioners snickered just a bit as Aunt Kathy jumped to his defense. "My boy said it! My boy said it right! Good job baby! Good job!" I must give credit for support.

Yet, Jerry's hiccup was only the door to something much darker taking shape.

As usual, Pastor Keith got up to close the ceremony. No doubt, all members were feeling the presence of the Holy Spirit.

Had I followed Aunt Kathy's theological push, that flock would've been all mine.

But finally, Pastor Keith walked to the podium and took the church on a voyage. "Who would deny Jesus? What type of man convicts a righteous man? How did Jesus, the son of God, The Prince of Peace, and the King of Kings get nailed to a cross!

"Nooooooooo Wayyyyy," by the crowd! "Nooo Wayyy!"

Then Boom, the church went berserk! There was singing, dancing, and clapping happening all around! Nothing but shouts of "Amen, Lawd Amen" came and went from near and far. But they were not alone. I joined in the fray as well. The place was totally polarized to a single rhythmic beat. Without prodding, Little Tommy started to yell, kick, and twist on the rug. Meantime, the aisles overflowed with well-wishers while my view of events became restricted. Somehow, Mom and Jerry disappeared into that sea of madness. Still, Zion Gate Union was rocking and rolling right off the foundation.

After Jerry's big let-down, Aunt Kathy went unseen and unnoticed, and then resurfaced inside the circle surrounding the pulpit. No one had ever broken through, and she would be the first. Normally, security kept all lunatics away, but this time, it wasn't so. Aunt Kathy had succeeded where others had failed.

Immediately, the service came to a pause because Aunt Kathy landed on the back of Pastor Keith like a Bull-Rider. "Take me to Calvary! Take me to Calvary! I'm here, Lawd! I'm here," she screamed!" "I got him, Lawd! I got him! He's mine, Lawd He's mine!" It was a rude awakening to cracks in the armor around the Reverend. The Deacons, Ushers, and Junior Ministers were forced to spring into action and restored order at the altar. But, no one had to say it, Pastor Keith was never the same. He was broken and domesticated by my aunt.

On a smaller matter, Jerry was drenched in tears while shouting, "*It's Easter, It's Easter! Everywhere, Everywhere, It's Easter!*" The Recital was over, but Jerry had stolen another kid's rhyme.

Meantime, Pastor Keith was outdone and not able to continue. He wore a major look of disbelief. Somehow, his cape failed to deploy and protect him.

COLUMBUS COUNTY FAIR

Later, in the fall of that same year came this big humdinger.

Kids, animals, and adults came to this annual event, and so did Zion Gate Union Baptist Church. If Pastor Keith was in attendance, then Aunt Kathy was there as well. This was a grand county event that provided another opportunity to walk Jerry about like a rotary display. However, Aunt Kathy knew of our dynamics and made me tag along. Jerry was her "Ace" and me "the Sandbag." In other words, I was just in the way. Sad, but Tommy didn't get the nod. He required too much care and attention to be towed around. But Aunt Kathy could retrieve Jerry and me at a moment's notice. We were always available at her disposal. Truth be told, I only made the team because of my connection to Jerry. I knew how to make him talk, laugh, and challenge me in a footrace. Yes, he and I still had a bond and Aunt Kathy knew it. Just as important, I was more than capable of taking Jerry about the Fairgrounds without getting lost.

But, on-the-other hand, it was amazing how a showcase of regional farmers and ranchers with vegetables, fruits, and livestock on exhibit became a place for "Joyful Moments." Well, if Aunt Kathy was there, so was The Lawd.

All children got to see the bulls, cows, goats, horses, pigs, and chickens. But no, not Jerry and me. We had to follow Aunt Kathy around while she searched for other members of the church. Anytime was a good time for an old-fashioned revival, even at the county fair.

Meantime, there were Hog Calls, Frog Races, and Hot Dog eating contests for delight and entertainment. But as expected, Jerry and me got a different assignment. So, stealing away became my objective to counter my boredom of tagging alone. Yet, in order to get a reprieve from torture, required some patience, planning, and a Spiritual Moment. If Pastor Keith was on the grounds, it was only a matter of time before we got a release. However, it was best to liberate Jerry as well. Otherwise, my freedom wouldn't last for very long.

The plan was set. Once Aunt Kathy became moved or got distracted, Jerry and me would jet out in the opposite direction. But painfully, the going had been tough and laborious for some time. Nothing went my way for more than an hour.

Then, out of nowhere, followers of Zion Gate Union joined the scene. Good yes! But unfortunately, they fell into Aunt Kathy's heathen pit of sinners. They were none other than Deacon Hunter and Usher Skip Sanders. Aunt Kathy had more respect for goats and pigs than these two parishioners. Believe it or not, she pretended to connect for the purpose of praising The Lawd. It was "Hallelujah Decon Hunter" and "Praise the Lawd Usher Skip Sanders." It was non-stop, "Oh Heavenly Jesus" and "Hear me Lawd, Hear me!" Meantime, youngsters raced from stable to stable to see the best that Columbus County Ranchers and Farmers had to offer. But luck does come to the few. As we walked and searched for a sign, we stopped at a Porta-Potty. A strange but joyful noise was emanating from the inside. Suddenly, the music stopped. Aunt Kathy felt the urge for a Spiritual Mark. She pulled the brakes, waited nearby, and forced Jerry and me to endure the stench of other people's lunch. Eventually, the door came open, and a member of Zion Gate Union Baptist Church stepped out! Once again, another Christian not in high regard. "Holy Jesus, it's you, Sister Alice!"

"Yes, Sister Kathy, I just had to talk to him!"

"Well, Praise the Lawd."

Meantime, Jerry stood tall and upright while holding his breath and pinching his nose. At least, I played it down and took one for the team. But Jerry didn't acknowledge Sister Alice and continued to squeeze his nostrils and puff up his jaws. Well, I knew Aunt Kathy viewed Sister Alice as a Backslider and part-time Jezebel, yet opportunity was hitting us square in the face. Quickly, I took a shot. "Aunt Kathy, Jerry and me are going to The Toad 500. We'll be right over there," I said, while pointing in the distance. "Yes auntie, I want to see Mr. Kermit," said Jerry. "OK, but don't stay too long. Sister Alice and me will find Pastor Keith and get our blessing right out here."

"Yes ma'am," I said, while nudging Jerry to take off!

Well, it didn't take long for my brother to be the pooper. He kept asking for hot dogs, popcorn, and powder cakes and we weren't even out of Aunt Kathy's sight. Yes, I had money, but it wasn't for food. But stuffing Jerry's mouth was a small price to pay for a Break-a-way from my aunt.

Next, he complained about the Toad 500. Obviously, he wasn't catching on. "Jerry, I made up that frog thing! We needed something besides chicken and cows to throw Aunt Kathy off."

Jerry turned to me with abject disgust. "Lying to Aunt Kathy is a sin!"

"You're correct, big bruh!"

Needless-to-say, he was completely indoctrinated. No doubt, he was in the tank and drinking the juice but pissing it out as well.

Moving on, I bypassed the Livestock and headed straight to the arcade. The Pellet guns, Penny Toss, and Pin-Ball games were tops amongst things to do. But I got sidetracked by the lights, bells, and cheers coming from a Billiards table. The crowd noise over there was riveting and magnetic. My curiosity got the better of me. I stopped in my tracks and recalibrated my mission.

Well, that section of the park was nothing less than a human zoo. Spectators were roaring, screaming, and shouting as the players played. People were placing bets on a mouse that scurried across the table. I was innocent to gambling but it didn't matter. I was captivated and drawn to the money.

Pick a mouse, choose a slot, and Ka-Ching, the vendor had to pay. I saw lot of dollars exchanging hands. So, I studied the game before joining in. Stealing away was my initial goal but adding a few smacks to my stash became the new cherry on top.

However, something much more than money took center stage. The top dog walked away with a brand-new red bicycle that orbited above the roulette. Man, I never had anything that spectacular in my life. It was a no-brainer. But, to keep those lips of Benedict Arnold closed, it was wise to put Jerry in the game, too.

Well, for every quarter I won, I had to give back two of them. Little Slept-Rock kept losing all the money I was making. On-the-other hand, I still got recognition for my successes.

As the tournament unfolded, I kept winning and wining. To my surprise, I was stuck on a Heater! I really couldn't lose, but Jerry could! Yet, when it was all over, I was in the Champion Circle. I didn't make a lot of money, but I had a bicycle coming my way! Holy Cow! I was the first recipient at the Columbus County Fair.

As the workers lowered that two-wheeler, I was prepping for the camera. It was the crowning achievement of my short life!

There I was in the Winner Circle, so full of smiles and tears of joy when Aunt Kathy suddenly appeared in my sphere.

Yet, she wasn't alone. People from the television station and *The Columbus Gazette* were waiting to interview me. But Aunt Kathy was never one to go unnoticed. "Oh, hey there, boys! What's going on?" Immediately, I replied with true excitement and pure adrenaline in my voice. "Just give me a minute, Aunt Kathy!" No way I could hide my happiness! "Yes Jesus, Yes," I thought! Mind you, I was wiping my face, fixing my collar, and brushing my hair. I wanted those cameras to capture my good side.

Meantime, Aunt Kathy stepped beyond the ropes and spoke with the Vendor. "Did he steal anything?"

"Wow," was all I had! I wouldn't be grinning if they're taking me to jail!" Of course, I didn't say it! But I thought it! "Oh no! No ma'am," said the

Owner. "He's the champion of Columbus County Fair Grand Prize! We need a snapshot and he's free to go."

Strange, but Jerry was on mute until Aunt Kathy came on board. "He got a new bicycle! But I didn't get one," he shouted! Our aunt dug a little deeper. "What's going on here?" "He betted on rats, and he won," said Jerry. Man, if I ever needed a ride-or-die sidekick, it was then. Jerry wouldn't let up and made things much worse. "Aunt Kathy, I want a new bicycle too!" Then he started to cry. I was so outdone with that dude! I mean, we could have shared that thing. Regardless, Jerry was blowing it for yours truly.

Finally, Aunt Kathy chimed in with her death knell. "Nah, Nah, Nah, this's the work of the devil!" She turned to the Dealer, "Sir, take back your bicycle and give me his entry money! Just a bunch of mess! I can't turn my back on Satan! He got my boys out here gambling and shit!" I was emotional and stunned! I stood there with my jaw in my hands and said not a word. I couldn't understand her. Had the shoe been on the other foot, or Jerry's feet, the poor shit out of luck would've been me! I was totally dejected with disbelief for months to come!

After this event, I started collecting discarded bicycle parts and built my own. It was ugly as hell, yet it was all mine. Eventually, I named it Mister Frankenstein.

SLIDE, HAL, SLIDE

Going back to my baseball days, Aunt Kathy smacked me down for all of Columbus to see. After I learned the game, I was a staple on the practice field and a solid force at the plate. Nothing made me happier than being amongst teammates while trying to improve my skills.

However, those were the years when Jerry and me started to drift apart because of separate interests. Initially, our differences were not totally Jerry's fault. Aunt Kathy was driving a wedge with every chance she got. Still, I desperately tried to hold a relationship with my brother. However, Aunt Kathy was much too impactful for a small kid like me. It didn't make any sense at all. I was contending with a relative just to keep Jerry connected to Tommy and me.

It became useless. The arrogance had taken root. Jerry came to expect top billing whenever he and I were together. Of course, I thought he was nuts. He was my older brother and not the king.

Prior to Aunt Kathy's heavy hand, Jerry and me were brothers-in-mischief. He was never innocent. We either found shenanigans or created deviltry to engage in out of boredom or curiosity. But when things went awry, I was the only one being punished. It took far too many butt beatings for me to acknowledge being near Jerry was a hazard to my health.

But once I accepted my place, I turned to baseball. It became my first love. I got attention, accolades, and acceptance unlike any other entity besides school.

Yet Jerry wasn't feeling my new transformation. The little sunshine I received started to rival his standing amongst mutual friends. So Jerry kept Aunt Kathy in the know of my whereabouts. It really shouldn't have mattered, because I started keeping my distance from him and Aunt Kathy. All my acts of pretention and false excuses were no longer needed as far as I was concerned. I was nearly detached from Jerry in every way.

At first, the proximity of the church and the playground wasn't a real issue. But boy oh boy, was I wrong! The ballpark was about two blocks away from Zion Gate Union. The chaos from our events happened to disturb Aunt Kathy and her Prayer Partners. But sadly, I wasn't aware of those deep distractions. In my head, Zion Gate Union made Joyful noises and so did the people at the park. Well, our tournaments were just a scream and shout from Wednesday night Bible studies. Once again, I failed to acknowledge baseball as being unholy in the eyes of Aunt Kathy. As for me, I had few concerns. I was ignorant, free, and loving life. Sad to say, Jerry didn't like my new spark. He knew of my practices and game times. Yet, he didn't have to track me; he knew exactly where I was every minute of the day. However, it was me who was blind to his ploy of exposing me.

Whether my team won or lost, I was making inroads. The league had a senior umpire who oddly took a shine to me. He was distinctly known as the Air Boss. This guy was an ex-military Marine retiree, and it showed. Just hearing that moniker got him juiced up and ready for the games. The Air Boss was regimented like a drill sergeant. He was extremely tough and nobody to fool around with.

Actually, I didn't think he liked kids, and for many good reasons. One: Most of the players didn't care for him either. Two; He was blind as a bat and way past his usefulness. Three: I think he worked the games for revenge and not for money. Four: He loved to argue and was never wrong. Last and not least: He had his own Strike Zone. His sweet spot never matched what the players or fans expected. Truth-be-told, he probably knew all about the sports of Cricket, Hockey, and Lacrosse, yet very little about baseball.

Naturally, all the teams complained about his lack of consistency, but the league backed him anyway. Well, the players showed their discontent through mis-pronouncing his nickname and throwing errant pitches toward his head. Fortunately, those baseballs never made contact, but it added to his anger. Verbally, the fans were just as rude. They would roast Mister Air Boss from the minute he made a Bad Call to the second he left for home. However, I don't think he gave a damn about anybody's judgements or criticisms. He was indeed the Air Boss of the Baseball Park.

Just as weird, was the attention Mister Air Boss gave me during the games. Honestly, I was afraid of him and did my best to hide such fears. Plus, I wasn't built to argue with adults. Even in doubt, I kept my sentiments to myself. So, Mister Air Boss only saw respect and determination coming from me on and off the field.

Understandably, Mister Air Boss was never seen conversing with the players. But on rare occasions, he'd coached me at the Batter box. "Son, you swung at a high ball" or "Young man, step back a little." Those were comments he sent my way every now and then. But man, I loved and appreciated the insight. I was new to the sport, so accepting advice from a guru meant a lot to me. Those instructions definitely added to my sudden rise in the game.

Well, it wasn't long before Aunt Kathy was canvassing the park in search of my involvement in baseball. Of course, she deemed my participation as ungodly behavior. Lucky for me, I was never seen nor caught during her rummaging. Our games didn't take place until Bible studies were in session. Still, Aunt Kathy would leave a couple of New Testaments at the press box for public consumption.

Meantime, Mister Air Boss thought Aunt Kathy's crusades were out of place and kind of funny. Strange, but those were the only times I saw a smirk on the old man's face. Then, once she was out of sight, he'd return her books to me. Luckily, neither Mom nor Aunt Kathy noticed the large stack of Bibles hidden under my bed. However, one day Mister Air Boss made an odd remark. "Son, one of these times you're going to strike out." I didn't know how to take his statement, or what he meant at all. I was solid at the plate even though far from perfect. yet, somehow, he managed to omit Aunt Kathy promised to return with Pastor Keith. Apparently, she swore to deliver the Holy Scriptures to all sinners in the stands. Well, that was needed to know information. If I knew anything, I knew Aunt Kathy would stick by her word. Especially if it had anything to do with distributing The Good Book. Unfortunately, Mister Air Boss didn't value her pledges the way I would have.

So, there I was, preparing for the biggest contest of my young life. It was U M Baptist East, my team, versus Alpha Alpha Alpha. We were the underdogs by a long shot for that contest. However, that squad had never faced me with big chips on the table. Yes, I was cocky and certain for the moment. On the other hand, I had so many expectations placed upon my shoulders. Even Jerry knew this event was big. Strange, but on the day of the big game, he left the house sooner than normal. I suspected he wanted to arrive early and claim a real good seat.

The ballgame just happened to be on a Wednesday night. Yes, it was the same day for Aunt Kathy's Bible class, but all the stars appeared to be aligned. After all, we were playing at our regularly slotted time. So, all things were good.

As soon as the game kicked off, I came to realize I was in way over my head. The competition was far greater than any level I'd ever taken part in. Alpha Alpha Alpha was just a class above my team in every imaginable way. Quickly, they jumped out to an early two to one lead like it was nothing. It wasn't long before I realized my giddy-up had gotten together and left town! Mind you, I was throwing as hard as I possibly could, but those guys kept bouncing me all over the park with such ease.

On offense, I was lucky enough to get on base with a bunt, but then came an error, before I delivered our first score. But Alpha Alpha Alpha wasn't falling for that hit and run trick for a second time. I was so out of gas. Even more troubling, my teammates didn't provide anything to our total. But the fans kept imploring me to make something happen. "Come on Hal, give em Hell!" The crowd was relentless. They were demanding blood from a turnip because Alpha Alpha Alpha depleted all the fight I had. Still, I kept pushing myself. I didn't want to say it, but a moral victory was good enough for me. Winning just wasn't in the cards on that very day!

Then suddenly, I got another chance at bat in the fourth inning. The contest was still locked at two to one with us being the team behind. All hopes of beating the champions had to happen right then and fast. As expected, the audience roared loudly for something grand. Of course, I heard them all. No, they couldn't be ignored because people were standing, seats were swaying, and metal chairs were clanging to the beats. "Let's go dude! It's you man, it's you!" Weird, but I searched the bleachers for my big brother. I needed a kindred spirit to get me going once again. Anything in the form of "a thumbs up," or "two hands clap," or "raised fist" could have ignited my fire. But for good measure, I prayed for luck and a new way to get it done. Most players had their families and friends on hand, yet I only had Jerry. But on-the-other hand, I never really knew my brother's true allegiance.

Looking back, Jerry established a pattern of following my tournaments. He became very popular at the park. He was more than a face in the crowd. Yet, I didn't recall seeing him before or during our shootout with Alpha Alpha Alpha.

Meantime, I looked over my shoulders and Mister Air Boss had a look of disappointment. Yes, I was stinking up the joint. I wasn't performing anywhere near my previous standards. Yet, the heckling from the crowd and superior stars on Alpha Alpha Alpha made me look average at best.

Weird to say, but I didn't want to disappoint the old grump behind the plate. So I dug in hard and deep at the Batter Box. If that pitcher took me down, then it had to be from something wicked, nasty, and out of this world. It was going to be either him or me. I wasn't going out like a wuss. Yet, things weren't looking good for The Mighty Other One. Then suddenly, all the marbles fell completely on me! Mister Air Boss yelled, "Full House!" That meant I was one strike from being out or one ball away from keeping hope alive. I was sweating like a criminal and scared to peek over my shoulder, yet I had to reclaim my pride. I steadied myself and begged the Lord for a ball to make good contact.

Unbeknownst-to-me, the pitcher for Alpha Alpha Alpha had studied my habits. Next, he threw a devilish curve ball that forced me off the plate and landed in the Catcher's glove for strike three. That was awful! I got caught looking like a deer staring in headlights! I'd struck the hell out. Well, I wanted to do good things, but I was treated like a bass boat to a Tsunami. Looking bad was an understatement. However, our fans showed support by staying silent. I really didn't know why, but it did soothe some of my pain. Hope had certainly left the arena. I lowered my head in defeat and turned toward the dugout. I'd let my team down. I disappointed the Southside Park. I lost a chance at glory. For the first time in my young career, I started to doubt myself. "That's Ball Four," said Mister Air Boss!

"Oh, what did he say? Am I hearing what I think he said?" My heart was racing! I wasn't sure, so he needed to repeat himself!

"Son, take your Walk!" Mister Air Boss shouted that command like a Drill Sergeant!

So, I threw down my bat and glanced back at the old man. I had nothing to say! I wasn't even sure he was serious. Mister Air Boss didn't say a word either. He just winked at me and pointed to First base. I was ecstatic! I was revived! Alpha Alpha Alpha was going to get more than a cheap ass bargain! I sprinted to base number one like a scared Warthog! It was on! Sadly, the opposing fans and followers took it out on Mister Air Boss. Even though the chorus continued for me, the biggest noise came from the rival's crowd sitting near our dugout. They were hot and angered because I was rewarded an opportunity I didn't deserve. Oh well, it was water under the bridge to me. I saw it as the beginning of better things to come. If Alpha Alpha Alpha continued to dwell about my freebie, then an avalanche of problems was sure to follow. Meantime, it was rough for the umpire. Immediately, a steady flood of "AIR HEAD and Mister AIR HEAD" were echoing throughout the park. It was chaotic like never before. Streams of AIR HEAD were loud and very easily heard.

Yes, I was glad to be in the game and still in the mix. But I knew I had a debt to pay. Mister Air Boss knew me only at the park. For reasons unknown, he put himself in a volatile position just for me. Damn it, I had to make the most of that mulligan. It wasn't about U M Baptist East and Alpha Alpha Alpha anymore. I couldn't allow a gift to slip through my fingers. Before Alpha Alpha Alpha accepted the umpire's bad decision and moved on, I was standing on second base like I owned it. Yep, I stole it like a thief in the night. Amazing, Mister Air Boss ignored all the chatter and took interest with my progressions on the field. I felt good but it still wasn't enough. My team needed me to score. One more point and the game would be even at two. My intent and desire were to touch down safely in front of Mister Air Boss. I owed that old man and wanted to make him proud.

Next, I took a deep breath and dove in the dirt while taking Third. I was too afraid to look up! Then, I heard the call! "He's safe," said the referee! Whew! Finally, I was closer to my goal. I was only 60 feet away from home plate. Yes, the visiting team, fans, and Haters were still bitter about my perk, but the game had changed. However, they weren't letting up. AIR HEAD, AIR HEAD, AIR HEAD! That racket kept reverberating back and forth like a cat walking on a piano. The more they chanted, the more annoying it became. They really hit a crescendo of "AIR HEAD, AIR HEAD!"

"Man, I got to repay Mister Air Boss for this insanity!"

All I needed was a wild toss from the Pitcher or a Pass ball by the Catcher, and I'd get home safely. Nothing short of a collision at the plate by the Catcher was going to stop me. As far as I was concerned, victory was well within reach.

My confidence had returned and so did the excitement of U M Baptist East. Meantime, no one noticed Aunt Kathy had entered the park carrying a broomstick. I mean, not a soul was alerted to her incursion. She was the definitely the big Red Elephant in the room.

Then, out of nowhere, the Catcher threw the ball long and wide in his attempt to tag me out. Without hesitation, I sprung up and hauled ass like a NASCAR finalist! Breaking even, with Alpha Alpha Alpha was just a few feet away. Understandably, the cheers went off the charts. I was about to bust hell completely wide open. Then suddenly, the most bizarre dilemma came before me. I was still a long way from home-plate but received immediate instructions like, "Slide Hal Slide! Get Down boy, Get Down!" But my coach, MJ

Hunter, wasn't the guy delivering the orders. It was Mister Air Boss. I couldn't help but feel an enormous lack of understanding. Yeah, he'd been helpful many times before, but this was a different matter. The team skipper was my boss on the field. Ignore him and I'm off the team. Meantime, Mister Air Boss had a face filled with stress and consternation as he implored me to follow his commands. Foolishly, I chose to disregard those directives because my coach controlled the flow and took top priority. Well, that was such a poor decision on my part. Like a hailstorm on a tin roof, I found myself being attacked by a large broomstick in rapid succession. It was Aunt Kathy spearing me down like a pissed-off Sorceress. It was Whack after Whack and Smack after Smack in the name of God. She beat me from head to toe, Butt to belly, and front to back. I got her sermon in the process. "I warned you to stay your ass away from here! Just a bunch of heathens with fuss and damnation!"

In the middle of being pummeled I couldn't help but think, "A broomstick, OK, but I was never restricted from that park! Next, she promised to minister the crowd, yet I became the target! Last, where in the hell was Pastor Keith and those Bibles?" It was so obvious her vows had turned to lies, lies, and more lies!"

Eventually, I got up and scrambled away. U M Baptist East went on to lose by a score of six to one and never challenged Alpha Alpha Alpha for superiority ever again.

OH, WHEN THE DEVIL GOES MARCHING IN

As Zion Gate Union Baptist started to grow, so did the popularity of the Youth choir. Because of Aunt Kathy, Jerry and me got inserted even though neither of us could sing. However, all members of the group knew I couldn't hold a tune. But I was good at faking it. Singing just wasn't my thing. I hated being there and always felt out of place. But occasionally, Jerry and I were given roles that put us front and center to some of the biggest concerts.

On the other hand, my desires changed when The Twins came aboard. These ladies were not ordinary. No, they weren't your garden variety or generic pair of teenagers. They were the same tag-team that jolted my world at the start of grade school. That's right! It was Mary and Martha. They were 14 years old, and I was 11. Yet I wasn't alone; all the guys saw them as fresh fruit on the vine.

Meantime, I was the sole recipient of physical and mental abuse. OK, maybe I poked the bears far too often and deserved their wrath and fury.

Well, it was extremely difficult being near without engaging them. Man, I wanted their friendship and attention. But respect and fondness came with a price, and I paid dearly. I got pushed, shoved, slapped, hit, kicked off my seat, and through the door while attempting to cozy up. Yet, it didn't matter. I had to break the ice. But unfortunately, a jackhammer wasn't going to crash through that wall. Still, I cherished all my bruises.

Because of prior history, I had some advantages. The Twins were notorious for dishing out assaults and bashing heads on the regular. They were gorgeous but pure Spitfire. They had no interest in boys, not to mention youngsters with my reputation. Yet all the guys gawked at them anyway.

But even more troubling was the fact their rages weren't the only source of concern. They had four delinquent siblings on standby ready to defend their honor. NS, LB, KC, and HH were truant bad asses without full monikers. They took it easy on the alphabet and only required a few letters for recognition. However, their victims failed to receive the same type of leniency. Well, The Twins put me through the wash and rinse cycle so frequent and often, the brothers probably gave me a pass due to some benign pity.

Whenever these ladies got upset, they fought like killer-bees to a honeycomb. They would swarm from opposing sides just to confuse you. Not only did they beat you, but they also left a mark. So, none of my peers dared to mess with them. They left all insults and scars to little old me.

Yet I took my beat-downs as a way of gaining ground. Needless-to-say, I thought I had a prayer of a chance, so The Twins were my mission from day one to the very end.

During my approach, I didn't use weak clichés such as "Hey good looking" or "Honey, how are you!" Shucks, I made up my own. My compliments were "Don't Dare to Double Down," or "I want the Daily Double," and "Two Scoops for me." Sad to say, the girls never found me funny or appealing. They kept me at a distance with overt threats the like of, "Boy, we'll knock your block off and put it on backwards" or "We'll put a hole in your head like a bagel." Never-the-less, that hostility became extra spice for a dream two-piece snack-pack. Even though I was bigger and older than our elementary encounters, I still couldn't tell them apart. However, I had bigger obstacles. Aunt Kathy promoted Jerry like an agent for change. Yes, he was their age, and I was only eleven, but he had no character or charm for these untamed broads.

Aunt Kathy would engage the girls in conversations just to feel them out. She even dropped suggestions, "Ladies, Jerry is the sugar and cream." Rats and double rats! She always destroyed my game and exposed my decoys.

Mind you, she didn't stop just there. Aunt Kathy piled it on with sweet surprises. She bought bakery items for the choir and then got Jerry to past them out. I became insanely jealous. He got all the close-ups, smiles, and googly eyes, versus the sneers, snide remarks, and dissed to the face I received.

OK, Jerry had an envoy in the choir. But it was still two sisters and two brothers. I knew Batman had Robin, "The Boy Wonder," so Jerry had me, "The Mighty Other One." Of course, that was only wishful thinking. My brother was an Opposer, not an ally. However, I knew my Aunt Kathy. She had something more adverse in the making.

Zion Gate Union Youth choir started to rival the popularity of Pastor Keith. Other sanctuaries recognized that claim to fame as well. We got summoned for Sunday school, Day service, Midnight Mass, and area churches around town. We didn't have to say a word, but expectations always ran off the charts. Our followers added to that suspense through chants of "Oh Yeah, Oh Yeah, Zoom Zoom Zoom," before, during, and after every performance.

However, the Youth choir truly was legit. We got the church spirited, emotional, and ready for a sermon whenever called upon. Then, right before Pastor Keith's final word, we closed with, "Let us Sing, Let us Dream!" Trust me, the place would rock and rattle off the hinges until the edge of darkness!

Well, everything kicked off once Jerry shouted out the Intro, "Hey everybody, Let Zion Gate Union Rise Again!" Next, The Twins followed while singing a medley of famous gospel hits. The crowd loved it. They consumed every bit of that showcase. It never failed. People were mesmerized through kids praising God, vocals from The Twins, and lectures by Pastor Keith. It all came together for good and spurn one big celebration. Yes, church services always ran late and way off schedule, but no one cared.

Furthermore, Christians came from all over the state to our events. No doubt Zion Gate Union was the envy of all surrounding churches. Every year, a concert was held to determine the Best Choir of Columbus, Mississippi.

The winner held the trophy for an entire year or until defeat. Fortunately, our choir was champions for the past two cycles.

Meantime, that big day was vastly approaching. There had to be at least 20 churches slated for participation. Yet I was scared and excited at the same time. I didn't want to mess up or be exposed for my lack of skills. On the other hand, I got gobs and gobs of quality time around Mary and Martha.

But all things weren't golden. Aunt Kathy manipulated her way into the lead role. That move created friction from the director to the pulpit to the congregation. Everyone, and I mean everyone, knew she couldn't hold a tune. Not to mention, she had no business in the Youth Choir. Aunt Kathy happened to be the only adult amongst the singers. She stood out like boobs on a bull. The group really had no use for her. Because of her presence, any hopes of gaining on The Twins went out the window. Even more important, Aunt Kathy altered the number of duets performed by Mary and Martha. The Twins were the backbone of the choir. They were the real deal and Zion Gate Union's secret weapon.

Naturally, the sisters' admiration for Aunt Kathy took a sour turn. They started to refuse all pastries out of resentment. It was obvious, Mary and Martha had been used. Because of Aunt Kathy's deceptions and deceit, I got the stinky eye at rehearsals, during church, at school, and on the streets. Before everything went to hell, I was getting a smirk and a nod here and there. Inroads to friendship didn't appear that far away. Plus, I foolishly thought I was wearing the sisters down. But after Aunt Kathy seized control, I was forced to enter a Protection Protocol. It was only a matter of time before frustrations came back to bite me in the rear end.

Aunt Kathy went further and changed all arrangements. She became more than a featured performer. She was calling the shots too. Our Closer, "Let Us Sing, Let Us Dream," a duet with The Twins, was immediately tossed out. Of course, this was the source of the real issue. I had a bigger role than my brother. I actually lead that hymn, "*Let us Love the Precious Things, We know our Christ is King, Come my way with sunshine, Come my way with rain, Let us Sing, Let us Dream, in your Holy name!*" That song was a knockout punch and the nail in the coffin to all Challengers. It was more impactful than our opener, "Let Zion Gate Union Rise Again."

Mind you, the audience would clap, jumped up and down, and joined in the chorus well before the second verse. Sad, but Aunt Kathy shit-canned our "Ace" and replace it with "Mary and Martha Got the News," without consulting with our Music Director or The Twins. Somehow, she thought her choice was the perfect hook because of the biblical connection. Yet the sisters despised her reversal. They didn't care for the correlation or the song. Yes, my duty got reduced to being a Presenter just like Jerry, but I was OK with it. I was a team player and only there for the grace of being. But unfortunately, the girls were spot on about a bad taste of symmetry. I wasted no time using those hymns as an opportunity to flirt, serenade, and get a rise out of them. Yet I wasn't alone. Other members would hum those lyrics as well.

None-the-less, The Twins complaints fell on deaf ears. Aunt Kathy carried way too much water at Zion Gate Union. Because of those adjustments, I became the natural outlet for discontent. My relationship with The Twins, which was fragile from the start, suddenly turned to trauma on a day-to-day basics. My hidden euphoria was oozing out of my pores at a record pace.

During rehearsals, The Twins sent arrows of death through cockeyes and stares. It was more than a bluff. I had another ass whipping waiting for me and I knew it. Without a doubt, those sisters didn't want anyone reciting the new lyrics. But I said them anyway and right on cue. It was an easy decision because I feared Aunt Kathy far more than The Twins. So, it was "Mary and Martha Got the News" whenever called on. Well, my flirting became more offensive in every sense of the word. Clearly my prospects of grandeur fell through the toilet. But there was no way to avoid The Twins renewed hatred of me. Still, I tried to ride it out and pray my remaining days weren't numbered. But it never pays to play with fire.

Unfortunately, there was nothing I could do. I was stuck in the middle of a cesspool. Quitting the choir was not an option either. Aunt Kathy would've beaten my pants off if I attempted to do so. On-the-other hand, the girls had something in store that wasn't to my liking!

Life became a living hell, whereas Aunt Kathy was knee deep in pigs galore. She was loving it all. Winning "The Best Choir of Columbus" really didn't matter. She had control and that was everything she wanted.

As for me, threats of being choked out came daily. Somehow Jerry was exempt. To be honest, he never pestered the girls the way I did. Because of those new elements, I wanted to switch positions with my brother. But of course, it wasn't that simple. I'd dug my own grave. It was only me with a target on my head. Yes, I was devastated. My come-ons with The Twins had gone so horribly wrong.

On the day of the concert for Best Choir of Columbus, Mississippi, all the greats showed up to claim that honor. There was UM Baptist East, Mission Helena, Southeast Spirits, Greater Tabernacle, and One Street Union just to name a few. Because of Aunt Kathy and dissentions amongst the troops, our expectations for victory went low and were certain to fail. Yet we had a reputation to uphold. As a measure of support, our followers still showed up to see Zion Gate Union retain its title.

The scene was set. We were scheduled to follow the Big Five groups listed above. Performing in the middle of the pack was a strategy that worked well for us the previous two concerts. It gave us recon and time to adjust as needed.

Usher Skip Sanders controlled the flow of the program. He made the introductions as each choir stepped into the church.

After the event got underway, there wasn't an open seat remaining in the house. Late-comers were forced to observe from the doors and near the windows. Anxiety in the crowd turned into pandemonium outside and inside the church. No one stayed seated after the opening act. All choirs created so much enthusiasm, it really didn't matter who song the lyrics, except for us. We had The Twins, and they were renowned all over the surrounding area.

Initially, all went as planned. There were no major surprises until Greater Tabernacle sang our Closer, "Let Us Sing, Let Us Dream." They did a good job, but it was nothing compared to us. We were consistent killers because of The Twins. OK, a few spectators got happy and caught "The Holy Ghost," but we usually stirred the entire house. Meantime, Aunt Kathy took offense. But it shouldn't have mattered. It was a defunct song. After all, she threw it out! Our new Closer was "Mary and Martha Got the News." Yet she was bitter and disturbed anyway.

Zion Gate Union never took a backseat to anyone. Yes, Greater Tabernacle was only showing some gamesmanship. They did our theme as a way of calling us out and putting everyone on notice. They wanted to send a message that winning wasn't going to be easy. The Zion Gate Union crowd had our backs and came forward with, "Oh Yeah, Oh Yeah, Zoom Zoom Zoom, Zoom Zoom Zoom, Oh Yeah, Oh Yeah, Zoom Zoom Zoom, Zoom Zoom Zoom!" That chant vibrated throughout the building. Some concert-goers joined in while opposing groups pushed back. But Aunt Kathy clearly lost it. She started cussing and accused Greater Tabernacle of stealing our anthem. Mind you, none of us were worried. It was just a shot across the bow and a form of flattery. However, that move did rev up the crowd. But we loved all challengers, whereas Aunt Kathy did not.

Suddenly, disarray and confusion created delays between performers. Aunt Kathy's attitude affected our psyche and added to our cause of failure. Not to mention, her barrage of swear words created even more embarrassment for Zion Gate Union.

All the ugliness unfolded in front of thousands of parishioners, fans, and concertgoers. I knew then my day wasn't going to end well. I had something coming I couldn't avoid. It was useless. The sisters were probably going to pound all the Salvation out of me at the close of the show.

Meanwhile, dozens of Prayers Partners attempted to console Aunt Kathy but to no avail. She wouldn't hear of it. Yes, I knew it was a waste of time. I knew she was threatened by Greater Tabernacle and didn't want to follow their big production. Yet, she fooled no one.

Finally, Aunt Kathy relented, but only after Pastor Keith stepped in. It appeared to be a blessing for the choir. His intervention brought back the duet "Let Us Sing, Let Us Dream," with The Twins. I was stunned to see Aunt Kathy yield without a fight. But unbeknown to everyone, including myself, a pandora's box had been opened. There wasn't a dumpster in Mississippi large enough to contain her rage and fury. But in the interim, things were looking up for The Youth choir. No doubt, The Twins were going to blow the roof off the building. With any luck, I might return home with the same body-parts I left with.

Usher Skip Sanders made the call for Zion Gate Union to enter the church and take the stage. Right on prompt, I blasted through the doors on the left side while Jerry led the choir on the right. "Hey everybody, Let Zion Gate Union Rise Again!" It was the perfect choice. We were determined to rebound from our big fiasco. The Twins garnered all attention from the moment they became visible. They were poetry in motion. It was hard to imagine such treachery inside those songbirds. Their voices could charm the devil, but not my aunt.

But, on that day, it was only Aunt Kathy carrying a scowl. She just wasn't letting go. She was still upset about Greater Tabernacle doing our big number. But no one cared! We had The Twins and dog-gone-it, we were OK.

As we marched toward the pulpit, Aunt Kathy purposely stayed out of rhythm. She had that look of not giving a damn. Of course, I knew her off-beats were intentional. Still, no one cared. All ears followed The Twins. It was their show, and it was on!

On stage, Aunt Kathy kept adjusting her robe. It was only a ploy to gain more attention. Meantime, Jerry stood on her left side and The Twins on the right. I was further down but next to the girls. That put me a safe distance from Aunt Kathy but too close to my soon-to-be assassins.

Suddenly, Aunt Kathy eyeballed the Music Director then signaled for "Mary and Martha Got the News." She had gone completely rogue. After agreeing with Pastor Keith and The Music Director to return "Let us Sing, Let us Dream" as the Closer, she chose to abort that plan just because she could. Mind you, we all agreed to answer the dare laid down by Greater Tabernacle. That kind of audacity was much too big to ignore! Yet our choir was forced to whimper and perform something that sowed hard divisions amongst the troops. This time, I was really stumped and surprised. Immediately, shockwaves rippled throughout the group. Everyone peeked at one another then beamed anger my way. They all acted as if I had something to do with my aunt's decision. Of course, I'm thinking, "Why, God why? Didn't we have enough trouble from the start?" However, Aunt Kathy was throwing her insanity around! Damn and double damn!

Next, my aunt turned toward me and motioned to start the song. Of course, I was scared but I wasn't stupid enough to disobey. If push came to shove, I could outrun The Twins. But Aunt Kathy knew where I lived. It was painful, but once again the choice was easy.

I ripped into the hymn, "*Mary Got the News!*" Then Jerry followed, "*But Mama Got the Blues!*" No one heard the slur, so I kept singing and looking forward. The choir joined in and revved up the vocals. Finally, the lyrics reverberated back to Aunt Kathy. Weird, but she went off script. She started screaming, shouting, and calling on high. That wasn't part of the show. Totally without notice she went straight to chorus then ad lib with her holiness. "Oh Mary, Oh Mary, Oh Martha, Oh Martha! HaHa! HaHa! Can you hear me, Lawd, can you hear me?" Her hands flew up and Aunt Kathy fell over backwards. In the process she took down one of The Twin sisters. The concert came to an abrupt stop while well-wishers looked-on in distress. That was no accident, and I knew it.

Usher Skip Sanders and the Crew rushed the stage for assistance. The injured sibling got removed, yet Aunt Kathy remained seated. It was all surreal but not beyond my aunt!

Our shot at winning was slim from the beginning, but suddenly, turned to just saving face. Yet, the show had to continue. With nothing left to lose, I snuggled up to the remaining Twin sister, nodded to The Music Director, and blurted out, "Let Us Sing, Let Us Dream." A loud gasp first came from the choir and then the audience too. I knew I was departing this world, so why not please somebody besides my aunt? Still, nothing happened except the crowd shouted back, "Come on y'all! Do that Thang!" The remaining half of the sisters tried to move farther away; however, I stayed closer than arm length. Yet she wanted nothing to do with the choir because of the incident with Aunt Kathy. But it was "Go time." For her it didn't matter. She continued to elbow and pinch my arm with all her might. Yes, I totally understood that anger. Our choir had been sabotaged. Still, I swallowed the pain and remained nearby. Out of habit, she returned her version of the death stare, but I ignored that arrow too. Yep, I knew my existence was slated for the frying pan. But someone had to take one for the team. For a second time, I blurted out, "Let Us Sing, Let Us Dream!" The lone Twin sister peered back into my eyes and then suddenly picked up the tune. She really sung her heart out. I took further initiative with the clapping of my hands and stomping of feet. Even Jerry got on board. Once the audience joined in, our Youth Choir turned it up and went acapella. It wasn't long before people started passing out and praising the Lord. At the end, it was nearly impossible to leave the building. People were hugging and giving High Fives on the way out. It felt so good to recover the way we did.

Outside, the choir gathered in the parking lot. We were exuberant and still embracing one another. The team that nearly fell apart came back together like champions. To everyone amazement, we finished in first place once again!

Luckily, no one was blaming me for Aunt Kathy's behavior. I gained respect of all my choir members.

Even the injured Twin sister came up and shook my hand. She went a bit further and kissed me on the cheek. She said, "Boy, you did good!" No doubt I gave a gigantic smile that covered all my face. "But you got to stop hitting on my sister," she said! I conceded my advances for that moment. Yet, I was twice as confused. I had no way of identifying the girls. I really didn't know which sister I'd been flirting with!

Last and not least, Aunt Kathy showed up with Usher Skip Sanders walking in her vacated steps. She was not in the best of moods. Her temperament was somewhere between a bucking bull and a rabid dog. No one needed to warn me. Yes, bad things were on the horizon. In my attempt to resume our concert, I failed to continue with "Mary and Martha Got the News." That was her personal selection. However, I made a gut call just to get things back on course. I couldn't stomach another minute of her dysfunctions. On-the-other hand, that judgement was about to take years off my rear end.

Well, Aunt Kathy made a beeline toward little old me. Mind you, she didn't bother to congratulate any members of the choir nor the lone Twin sister. She wanted me in the worst way! Most of the group opted to take off for shelter rather than witness the wrath of my aunt. My teammates didn't know much, but they knew outrage!

So, there I was, standing with The Twins while Aunt Kathy, Jerry, and Usher Skip Sanders closed in. Aunt Kathy wasted no time reading me the riot act. She accused me of overstepping my bounds and showing off at church. According to her calculations, "I needed to get my ass snapped back in shape"! Then she said, "Don't worry, I plan to cut you a "New Ass" when we get home!"

"Yes Ma'am," I said. It was just another day in paradise! Yes, I knew I was cooked. I was finished.

Aunt Kathy continued. She wanted to break me in front of Jerry, Usher Skip Sanders, and The Twins. But if anyone needed a miracle, it was me. Suddenly, Usher Skip Sanders chimed in, "Sister Kathy, everyone loved the group. Our choir was invited to four more concerts within the next two months. People want to see The Youth Choir perform at their place. Your nephew and that Twin girl left them spellbound. If I were you, I'd give your nephew a break and a Big Mac." "Uh Huh! You don't say," said Aunt Kathy. "All these invitations are a blessing for Zion Gate Union." However, I knew she didn't respect Usher Skip Sanders enough to make a difference.

Then it really happened! "Heyyy, there you are! Young man, I've been searching all over this building!" It was Pastor Keith. "I got to thank Sister Mary and Martha too! You ladies pulled something out of those Christian folks today!" Obviously, he couldn't identify the girls either. Then Pastor Keith turned back towards me. He saw my puffy eyes. I was trying to hold some dignity in front of the girls. Yet Aunt Kathy had chipped away most of it. "Brother Hal, you should be smiling, rejoicing, and dancing up and down the streets of Southside!"

"Yes sir," I tearfully said. "Sister Kathy, we got to keep this one."

"Amen, Amen, Reverend. That's my "Other" nephew, Pastor Keith! I'm so proud of that boy," said Aunt Kathy.

"I want to see y'all this Wednesday at Prayer service. I like what you're doing, Sister Kathy." Next, he walked off with a huge grin on his face.

Once the Reverend was out of sight, Aunt Kathy eyeballed me up and down with a frown more terrifying than ugly on an ape. My life still hung in the balance. As much as I tried, I couldn't hold my emotions any longer. She started up again, "Boy, for a minute, I was really scared for your ass! But I'm gonna let you slide this time!"

"Yes ma'am," I said.

She went even deeper, "You may have slipped through the cracks, but if I catch you taking a shit out of turn, I'm beating your ass!"

"Yes ma'am," I said once again.

"I'm taking Jerry for ice cream. Would you girls like some too?" The Twins peeked at me, yet knowing I wasn't invited. They smirked at each other out of disbelief, and then stated, "No ma'am, we need to get home. Hal, see you on Prayer Wednesday." Just like that, the girls vanish in the same direction as Pastor Keith. I was somewhat ecstatic and relieved! Whew, I made friends with the hot chicks of Zion Gate Union. Of course, I had no plans to stop flirting.

COLUMBUS GOT TALENT TOO

At age 12, I was drawn to the Boy Scouts like toads to a Lilly Pad. Once I saw the kids and drills in the Christmas parade, I knew where I wanted to be. I loved the attention, structure, formations, and camaraderie within the ranks. Yes, it was a challenge, but I had to try. I wanted to wear those military fatigues, too.

Sure, I wore suits to church and outfits on the baseball field. But, there was something majestic about the Boys Scout uniform. That outfit said it all. There were caps, tassels, badges, ribbons, and medals to decorate your arms and shoulders. Oh my, I couldn't wait to dress up in full regalia. So naturally, I became determined. In my head, Southside needed a Little General like me.

But first, I had to make the squad. Being accepted was a struggle. Living in the poorest community created an extra obstacle. Boys from the Trash Alley and the Red-Line didn't fit the caliber they recruited. Most people avoided or stayed clear of kids from my side of the tracks. Second, I needed a uniform. Problem was, I didn't know any Boy Scouts at all. So, I had no dibs on leftovers or hand-me-downs. Yet somehow, I had to find another way.

The Columbus Jamboree at Propst Park was vastly approaching. Surprisingly, The Southside unit had been invited to fellowship alongside all other chapters. That event was going be the first integrated Boy Scouts and Cub Scouts alliance for the city. There was no way our director would allow me to participate without being in formal attire.

Meantime, it didn't take long to get established within the group. I was on time to each and every meeting. I recited the Twelve principles with ease: "A Scout is trustworthy, loyal, helpful, friendly, courteous, kind, obedient, cheerful, thrifty, **brave**, clean, and reverent." I was like a broken record. I had the Boy Scout's creed on recall at a moment notice. I became the Top-Dog at all fundraisers. I just had a knack for getting people to contribute to Boy Scout causes. I was the perfect guy for the mission. I was aggressive yet polite. I could explain our goals. I was charming and engaging. Lastly, I showed appreciation regardless of the outcome. It wasn't long before my success and spirited approach impressed the brass in my troop.

Scout-Master Allan knew I was a wayward kid and took me under his mentorship. Yes, I relished that attention and jumped at every opportunity to impress him.

Yet, I knew trouble wasn't far ahead. Aunt Kathy took issues with me being a part of events and organizations beyond Zion Gate Union Baptist church.

However, I wanted to break away from her webbing. I needed to do things that stimulated me.

Sadly, Aunt Kathy took Scout-Master Allan to task on several occasions. She argued, I had no business being around a bunch of frolicky mess. She stated, "The Lawd had something for me. This Kid Scout-in-the-Hood business was hindering my growth."

I can't explain it, but Mister Allan held firm and stayed supportive. He kept me on anyway. Somehow, he knew I needed them more than they needed me. Of course, I stuck out like a mule in the Kentucky Derby, yet I was determined to be a part of that group.

The Boy Scouts weekend consisted of building campfires, tying knots, and making Hobo stews. It was a great way to bond and burn off excess energy. I took full advantage of being outside with the guys. I was petting skunks, feeding buzzards, chasing snakes, and swimming with snapping turtles.

Yet, the big bash was just days away and I still needed a uniform. No outfit meant no Jamboree. My only hope was the thrift shops of Columbus.

Well, I didn't waste any time. The first chance I got, I raced downtown to try my luck and scavenge through the needy drop-offs.

Out of nowhere, I bumped into Aunt Kathy at the Salvation Army store. She was scrupulously searching for clothes that held their value. Shockingly, Aunt Kathy discovered the exact gear I badly needed. But she was determined to gift those items to Jerry. Gleefully, I tried to explain my dire situation. In return, she stated, "It shouldn't matter what you wear. A uniform is a uniform. By the way, I have that outfit in blue and it has your name on it. You'll look so handsome in that color. You do remember, I'm the one who put clothes on your back at the start of school.

"Yes Ma'am, I do."

"Boy, I know what I'm doing!"

Well, she had me there. After all, she did set me up in a Peppermint red shirt and Wintergreen polo for Mitchell Memorial Elementary. OK, I was grateful, but I couldn't back down. I was desperate! So, I pleaded and explained the brown apparel met all requirements for my unit. But Aunt Kathy didn't care for the words coming out of my mouth. "Honey, I know how to dress you. But Jerry needs these trousers to match his fishing outer-wear. However, I can see those Kid Scout-in-the-Hoods have you stirring up shit already."

I had nothing! I was crushed. Quickly, I realized I had only one possible option. Cut a deal with my brother and that uniform could be mine!

Just as promised, Aunt Kathy delivered the Brown G. I. Joe fatigues to Jerry. Of course, he was overjoyed. Putting on that outfit gave him a different definitive appearance. Yet, it happened to be the sculptured look I was shoot-ing for. None-the-less, I still needed that uniform for the Columbus Jamboree.

For whatever reason, I decided to try on the Blue Sailor outfit. Hell, it was just lying there, so why not. Weird, but that getup still had the badges, tassels, and insignias attached to it. Like magic, Jerry became fascinated by the way it made me shine and radiate in his presence. All the pomp, flash, and colors regained his interest. Immediately, he demanded a switch. Without haste I agreed for the change. Finally, I got what I needed!

On the day of the Columbus Boy Scout's Jamboree, I was as bold as a bald eagle. I stood out in the oddest fashion. My uniform didn't have any awards, frills, or bells connected to my clothing, but I was good. It was bland but the most gorgeous piece of clothing I'd ever worn. Being the lone trooper without any stripes didn't bother me. I had arrived and was loving the splendor of it all.

As we conversed with other cadets, I met a senior Scout leader with connections to the Uncle Donnie show. The guy was impressed with the style, character, and professionalism of the Southside unit. For reasons unknown, he promised to get our squad an evening slot with the local television station. I couldn't believe my ears. I wasn't sure if he was serious, but it sounded good. Every kid in Columbus dreamt of making that show. Uncle Donnie was very personable and had a gift for drawing Action figures right on demand. All the local Boy Scouts, Cub Scouts, Girl Scouts, Brownies, 4-H clubs, and other organizations had been invited; yet none had ever been African American.

Of course, I couldn't wait to share the news with the headmaster. Well, he didn't take me seriously. But later that week, he got the invite from Uncle Donnie himself.

Meantime, Jerry no longer lived at home with Mom, Tommy, and me. He would frequently stop by just to steal anything that gained his interest. On the way out, Jerry concealed our Kool-Aide, Goofy Juice, and Captain Crunch in his travel bag. He didn't give a damn whether we needed it or not. Whatever he wanted, he took with no apologies. With any luck, Jerry only stole fluoride from the toothpaste. But other days, he ran off with the Spam between your sandwich, icing off the cake, yoke out of the eggs, and sugar from the cookies.

If that wasn't enough, Jerry felt his Cub Scouts uniform was the source of bad luck. His past two fishing trips didn't yield any results. So, he demanded an immediate reversal of outfits.

Once again, I desperately tried to convince him otherwise. "Jerry, fishermen have bad luck all the time! Clothing has nothing to do with it." To my chagrin, he wasn't buying it. "Aunt Kathy asked about my brown outfit!"

Oh hell, I thought! "What did you tell her?"

"I told the truth."

"What do you mean by that, Jerry?"

"You stole my brown pants and shirt!"

"Say what! I did no such thing!"

"Well, she isn't happy!"

"Man, we made a deal!"

"But we didn't shake on it. So, I want my stuff back or else!"

Oh damn! Of course, "else" was code for Aunt Kathy, the Enforcer!

I was trapped. I was wedged between a crooked brother and evil aunt. No uniform meant no field trip to the Uncle Donnie show. My dream was fading and fast. I had to find another way to reach Jerry delight.

Suddenly, it hit me! Jerry wanted my record collection. He always did. He took an album here and there, but never found my cache. Time was ticking. The Uncle Donnie show started at four o'clock p.m. Live TV waits for no one. I was out of money with only one choice available. So, with pain and consternation, I traded my stockpile of Rhythm and Blues for Jerry's Boys Scouts brown uniform. He jumped at the chance to own my music like a hungry dog to a new bone.

With deep regrets, I parted with The Commodores, LTD, The Jacksons, Donna Summers, The ISLEY Brothers, The Temptations, and Motown's legend, "Aretha Franklin." They all vanished in a flash.

To me, Jerry won the lottery. Meantime, I didn't tell anyone about the Uncle Donnie Show. Why risk a fantasy being destroyed by Aunt Kathy.

Moving on, our unit got to the studio with time to spare. Once again, I wore my plain Brown G.I. Joe outfit. I didn't need badges, tassels, or insignias. My huge smile was bigger than any medal. Even Uncle Donnie noticed my glow. He shook my hand and gave me a Three Finger salute well before the show began. My head was on cloud nine and rising. The Boy Scouts were the place to be. At last, I was somebody! For the first time in a lifetime, I was going to be bigger than Jerry at Mitchell Memorial Elementary.

Strange, but the clouds creeped in, and rain shut down all outdoor activities in Columbus and the surrounding area. Of course, that meant lawn care, jogging, golfing, and fishing had to cease. Still, none of us cared. Uncle Donnie was our interest and entertainment. He kept us engaged, focused, and safe inside his comfy studio.

During the show, each cadet got interviewed and given a cartoon illustration as a parting gift. I couldn't wait my turn! I'd watched the program for years and wanted some personal memorabilia. Then boom, the moment arrived!

First, Uncle Donnie drew a sunflower and used my head as an avatar. Next, he asked about my professional ambitions. But I was caught off guard. Confusion and stage fright overtook me. No other trooper had been queried in that manner. I kept searching myself for something smooth and highly acceptable. I had affinity for so many different careers. But my aspirations were tainted by Aunt Kathy's own vison. To her, I was born to be a minister. She kept nudging me toward that direction. Sure, I witnessed the Fire and Brimstone of Pastor Keith like all other church members. No one could frame a story like the Reverend. To me, he was "The Esquire, GQ, and model of a man. He carried the Word of God with charisma and control. Once again, I saw it all. But preaching wasn't for me. I just wanted to find myself before attempting to direct others. For the record, I didn't know any ministers as colorful and effective as Pastor Keith.

But I stood frozen in a quandary. People in the studio and viewers at home became impatient, and aware of my nervousness. Suddenly, "a Lawyer! I want to be a Lawyer," I said. It all shot out in a high pitch.

Whew! I got a load off my chest and with any luck, those details went out during commercial break. My hesitation was certainly a bad look. But regardless of humiliation, I made The Uncle Donnie show! I was on TV. My status had to be higher than the day before.

As planned, my fellow mates got images created and signed. Shortly after that, the weather returned the skies to normal. So, we gathered our things, shook Uncle Donnie's hand, and then raced out the door. Unlike the rest of the scouts, I had two posters as souvenirs for the refrigerator.

On the journey home, Scout-Master Allan didn't stand a chance. He tried in vain to calm us down, but no way was it going to happen. Our enthusiasm didn't allow that Country Squire station wagon to touch the pavement. It was cloud 19 or bust for the rest of the trip. Everyone, and I mean everyone, couldn't stop overtalking the other Scout. Yet, comprehension was never an issue. Our hearts and emotions kept fluctuating somewhere between ape-shit and bananas. We were the epitome of insanity. Just a bunch of rowdy kids, trapped in an ugly car, traveling toward the Southside.

Previously, Mister Allan admired our behavior at the Boy Scouts Jamboree, but this was completely different, and he knew it. He wore a unique face of pride! To us, he was "The Man" and he'd done "a Great Thing!"

Within minutes of returning home, came a visit from Aunt Kathy and Jerry. Unfortunately, she didn't come to praise me. Still, I couldn't hide my happiness. I didn't even try to suppress my glee. "Hey, Aunt Kathy, I got these posters from the Uncle Donnie show!"

"Yeah, I saw you and that mess. I couldn't believe my damn eyes and ears! Liza, this boy got on television and fixed his mouth with a bunch of lies! Just lies, lies, and more lies! I got to tell Pastor Keith about this fool! Lawd, Lawd, he spends one month around those Kid Scouts-in-the-Hood and he's Backsliding already."

"Just pray for him, sister! Just pray for him! You know those Dead Dawgs and Haints are out there."

"Liza, if you say so. But the Lawd might be finished with him!"

Still quiet and out of sight, Jerry examined my drawings from the Uncle Donnie Show. I really needed him as a diversion, yet he had other ideas. However, I was forced to ignore Jerry and his investigations. Aunt Kathy was on the prowl, and I knew better. I wasn't going to turn my back on her for a split second. Becoming a mook-mouth little boy was still possible. But finally, she said what she said, and then walked out the door with Jerry.

The next day, Aunt Kathy took me to see the troop leader while Jerry took refuge at Mom's shack. She gave our director enough rage and bile to fill every toilet on the Southside. She called him every demonic name available and some I didn't know of. According to Aunt Kathy, Scout-Master Allan had steered me away from the Zion Gate Union Church. Being the son of Satan would've been a step up for my director.

As quickly as I reached the summit, I was back at the bottom of the pit. No one had to tell me to stay away. The embarrassment was much too great. The devil had spoken! My aunt's message was all too clear.

After humiliation and defeat, I rushed back to the house. Jerry was no longer around. But that wasn't unusual. Immediately, I noticed his blue Cub Scouts outfit was lying neatly across the bed. Yes, it was shocking for a fleeting moment, but it didn't matter. Just for the hell of it, I searched for my Brown G. I. Joe fatigues, but they couldn't be found either. It was such a waste of effort anyway. I was bounced out of the Boy Scouts of America for good. Somehow, that cut wasn't deep enough. As I walked into the kitchen, my sketches from the Uncle Donnie show had been taken. Amazing how my whole world flipped in the span of hours. But still in my heart I shall always be a Boy Scout in mind, body, and spirit. Forever, I remained, "Trustworthy, Loyal, Helpful, Friendly, Courteous, Kind, Obedient, Cheerful, Thrifty, **Brave**, Clean, and Reverent."

BACK TO THE EULOGY: GOING HOME

After exposing the real Aunt Kathy, I was able to rejoin Zion Gate Union Memorial service. Fortunately, my urge to toss my breakfast had greatly dissipated. Everything appeared on schedule and eventually I had to speak as well.

However, I noticed Pastor Keith altered his course. "For Christians, death is just a phase. Feel the warmth of Sister Kathy. She built this place! Her passions are the bricks. She got me in the door!

When we move her body, she'll still be here. This is her house, and it will always be. Can anybody hear me?"

"Yes, Reverend, Yes! Lawd have Mercy now!" said the congregation.

"We want that vibe to stay here and stay in this sanctuary! As I look around, I need more Sister Kathies. I want some Brother Kathies, too. Zion Gate Union needs that kind of spirit."

"Hallelujah Lawd, Hallelujah!"

I wasn't counting, but everyone got up to dance. Some bopped their heads, jumped up and down, and kicked in their seats.

"Can y'all hear me? I need folks ready for Church!" Ruckus and more ruckus engulfed the building! People sprung up again while raising their hands!

"I'm here, Lawd, I'm here," they said!

No doubt he had a witness. Pastor Keith smirked and waited as the volume turned down. Then he started up once more. "When the church needed lights, guess who?"

"Sister Kathy!" they said.

"When the kitchen needed heat?"

"Sister Kathy!" they said again.

No way he would get disappointed. "When the roof sprung a leak?"

"Sister Kathy!"

"When the bus broke down?"

"Sister Kathy!"

"When the mowers stop mowing?"

"Sister Kathy!"

"Don't y'all stop!"

Immediately, the gates swung opened at Zion Gate Union. "Sister Kathy, Sister Kathy! Sister Kathy, Sister Kathy!" That was all I heard.

"Preach, reverend Preach!" I said.

"When the Choir needed help? Y'all know!"

Well, that was a bridge too far. Whispers started and a chill came in. Aunt Kathy wasn't fit for a microphone, and everyone knew it. Yet Pastor Keith held his ground. He got them back by dancing, singing, and stumping on the stage. He knew his flock. After all, he was The Minister of Mississippi! Mocking the servants was all it took. Just like that, the fire roared back. "Sister Kathy had my back! What did I say? Sister Kathy had my back!"

Pure mayhem pours out! The church blew a gasket! "Kathy, Sister Kathy! Kathy, Sister Kathy! Kathy, Sister Kathy!"

Shucks, I started to yank my head to the rhythm. I went even further and drummed the casket. "It was Kathy, Sister Kathy, Boom Boom! Kathy, Sister Kathy, Boom Boom! Kathy, Sister Kathy, Boom Boom!" Weird, but The Car song played in my head. Yet, my beat, the cymbals, bongos, and tambourines really set it off. It was so invigorating. I was engulfed and really punishing that body crate. Then without warning, Pastor Keith pulled me in. "Come on Brother Hal! Talk to them folks! Speak to our servants! Reach out to our Christians! Go on son, go on now, just Preach!"

Wow, I was knee deep in the pulpit. I was on the spot and asked to deliver something out of nothing. Yes, I wanted in but had no fuel for that fire. Yet, there was no way to hide or flub a word. There was no thundering or lightening to cover my lies. Not a breeze, chirp, or sneeze in the air. It was all on me, the Preacher, with so little to share.

Quickly, I went back to clearing my throat. "Ahem! Ahem!" I wanted to keep it short. Yet somehow, I had to feed that hunger stirred by the Reverend.

Out of nowhere, came the urge to let go and live forward. So, I began to talk and nourish the congregation. "Aunt Kathy! Aunt Kathy, we miss you! We need you, now!"

I meant none of it. But it sounded really good. It made me look the part. Things started to roll my way.

Then without warning, Jerry and Tommy traded blows out on the floor! It was mano e mano. Next, they disappeared under the pews while locked in a free-for-all! It was the craziest shit I'd ever seen in a church. They moaned! They shouted! "She's, my aunt!"

"She's, my aunt!"

"No, damn it! You're a fool!"

"No, you're the fool!"

"Not yours!"

"Not yours!"

"She's mine!"

I was embarrassed, yet stoic and couldn't move a muscle. It was too much at a place I didn't care to be! But I knew bullshit and I knew phonies. Of course, this was both.

After the church got shocked and subdued, not a word was said. I had nothing for the actions of my brothers. Hell, I wasn't sure how I rank on their docket for beat-downs. So smartly, I stayed in my corner and kept my peace.

Finally, Usher Skip Sanders and the Crew got Jerry and Tommy separated and under control. They showed no remorse and didn't care to show any as well. It was their world and Zion Gate Union was only oysters in it. Just as damaging was my look of indifference. Honestly, I didn't care! I didn't care for that circus or the pair of hyenas!

Looking back, Pastor Keith's journey of remembrance neutralized my resentments. Feelings that ran hard, deep, and to the core suddenly seemed out of place. Regardless, there was work to be done, and I was still at the mic.

Before the Monday morning melee featuring Jerry and Tommy, the church was nearing the Holy Spirit. I had them in my hands. But now, I needed some real magic. Yet I wasn't a preacher. But it was far too late to realize such a thing. Then suddenly, I got an epiphany, a voice! "Just say it! Hal, go on and say anything!"

Unexpectantly, I lost all fear. So, with full confidence, I glanced at our servants, locked eyes with Pastor Keith, and said, "My Aunt Kathy wore a lot of hats! She was the blanket to Zion Gate Union!"

The crowd roared back! "Amen son, Amen! Say it Brother Hal! Say it! Take your time, Hal! Take your time, now! Gwon son!"

"She was the hope!"

"Yeah! Aright now! Come on Hal, Come on!" they said.

"She was a teacher!"

"That's it, son! That's it! Gwon now!"

"She was support, a builder, a ladder, and a beacon!"

"Yeah! Amen and Amen! Alright now, son, Alright!"

"I know and y'all know, that Zion Gate Union knew that God knew of her passion! Lord, let her in!"

Man, I didn't have to say another word. The place started rocking and came unglued! On the other hand, I couldn't believe what escaped my mouth or how my stomach stayed together. Yet the crowd wanted a little more! "Come on Brother Hal, come on! Tell em Brother Hal, tell em!"

Strange, I felt a sense of belonging and relished that attention. Shucks, I dove back in. "I want to serve the way she served! Ouch, Ouch! She gave and gave, but no pain, no gain!"

Suddenly, it was bonkers to bananas from wall to wall! Even confetti rained down. People bumped and bounced in jubilation. "Amen, Brother Hal, Amen! Hallelujah Brother Hal, Hallelujah!"

In the mist of celebrations came Jerry, "Aunt Kathy! Aunt Kathy, Lawd Aunt Kathy! I miss you! Lawd, I miss you!" That was par for the course. Once again, Jerry-come-lately tried to steal my Thunder.

But Tommy was finished. He left it all on the floor.

To my surprise, I became the show. I became the man fanning the flames as Pastor Keith watched in silence. He even stepped aside as the crowd rushed to touch, shake my hand, and pat me on the back. People continued to rejoice, dance, and stomp their feet in the isles. They screamed! They shouted! "We gonna miss her! Lawd, we gonna miss her! Lawd, have mercy on our sister!" Admittedly, I was thrown for a loop. It was a lot of love and much more than expected.

Unofficially, I'd crossed a "Line," and it showed. Pastor Keith didn't appear all too pleased. He stood tall and motionless while his eyes dissected me. My time was up, and I knew it.

Softly, I walked over and delivered him the mic. It was a good run. I wasn't the Opener, nor the Anchor of that eulogy.

Pastor Keith reached out and grabbed his baton with true grit and purpose! He was focused and determined! No doubt, he meant business!

Immediately, he stepped on the gas and released the nitro. He spoke with audacious fire unlike any time before! "We're still here, Sister Kathy! We hope you hear us too!" This was mighty and something different. It was more than a sermon! It was intense. Everyone grabbed a book and touched a hand. Scriptures bled out and hearts came open. "Y'all saw Jerry and y'all saw Tommy! It hurts when Good Folks lose Good Folks! But we know the Spirit! Somebody say Amen! Somebody shout for the Lord!"

Once again, the sanctuary leaped up and down, "Amen, Amen, Amen, Yes Lawd, yes! Oh Lawdy Lawd! Have mercy now!"

The Reverend picked up but zoned out in the process. He spurted sentences and phrases faster than ears could hear them. It was eerie and ghost-like. He became a figure-on-a-string. Pastor Keith veered right, struck a pose, shimmied his shoulders, and the crowd did likewise. Next, he turned left, pointed, and delivered the rest of his monologue. No one dared to move. They became locked in place like mannequins at the mall. But they were not alone. I was dazed, too. I desired something more. I wanted to get closer and embrace The Minister of Mississippi while he glorified the Lord. I wanted to feel that electricity. Yet, I was frozen. I couldn't make a sound nor move an inch. Strange, I'd never felt that way. I was right there, but so distant, too. It was so surreal! I saw embers fill his nostrils while he preached, seduced, and serenade the crowd with mere words. He sent Zion Gate Union through a spiritual awakening. The man was more than a Wizard. He was The Matrix. Obviously, he wanted to do something grand. He went even further! He exorcised the hate and hostility from the hearts.

Then finally, without notice, he brought it back down. "So many have Sister Kathy to thank! Go ahead Lord! Take her body but leave her soul! She's the soil of Zion Gate Union. She's the foundation! She's mother of the church! She's a gatekeeper!"

With extreme weariness, his tank ran low, and Pastor Keith was done. The spell was broken! Nothing but love and redemption fell upon the masses. People walked about giving hugs and kisses while dancing and shouting with tears of joy!

I felt so rejuvenated, but numb, too. Even Deacon Hunter, Sister Alice, and Usher Skip Sanders embraced one another. It was so ironic! They came to bury Aunt Kathy and bury her deep. Yet, emotions flowed unexpectedly amongst them. "Forgive us Lawd! Forgive us!" Yep, Pastor Keith fixed them, too. I was stunned! I had a renewed spirit. I wasn't harboring angst and resentments anymore. The reverend brought it home. He washed away the hurt. Wow, I never saw it coming. I was born again for a third time.

No doubt Aunt Kathy left a stain. It got bigger and darker when touched, but suddenly, it was gone. I felt a release. I couldn't explain it. Since forever, I was "the potty meat" to Jerry's "Prime Rib" because Aunt Kathy wanted it that way and that's how it had to be. But no longer did it matter. Quietly, I bit into my finger. I had nothing and felt so ashamed. Yet, the crowd continued as the noise moved on. I couldn't think nor feel my face. I was feckless.

Then suddenly, I regained my voice and purposely betrayed the Anti-Christ. "Leave my Aunt Kathy alone. She doesn't want you! Find someone else, Damn it!" The hate was gone and off my chest. Finally, I came back to full consciousness and found myself giving praises without being prompt. Wow, I couldn't believe it, but I was finally healed!

Unlike our Sunday service, Pastor Keith immediately signaled to the choir. So, The Twins rose like synchronized swimmers. They pivoted to the left and swiveled to the right in one smooth motion. They even wore the exact same dimple in the exact same region of their faces. They didn't need a mirror. If one had dirt on the jaw, trust me, the other sister had it, too. Once again, the girls threw me for a loop. One sister winked at me and then traded places with her twin. Just like the other times, I was left perplexed. I couldn't differentiate heads or tails in a police line-up. But luckily, Deya was my companion. In other words, my flirting had to end.

Without further delay, Pastor Keith pitched it back to me, so I led the exodus. No doubt, I still had it. Calmly, I belted out the opening lines, "*Let Us Sing, Let Us Dream, Let Us Love the Precious Things!*" The Twins took it from there. As expected, they were music in motion. Then, out of nowhere, Pastor Keith interrupted the choir. "Hold it! Hold it," he said!

Yes, I was afraid something had gone terribly wrong. Mind you, that was my preferred selection. Did I upset the reverend once more time? No, this time I was mistaken. He stated, "Today is filled with bountiful blessings! It's been a harvest. We are the seeds of Sister Kathy!" Then he sang the closing lines, "*We know our Christ is King, Come my way with sunshine, Come my way with rain, Let us Sing, Let us Dream, in your Holy name!*"

Right on cue, the pallbearers stepped in and carried Aunt Kathy out.

ASHES TO ASHES

The ride to the cemetery was just as empty as the drive over. Just like before, only Deya and me shared the limousine, whereas Jerry and Tommy deliberately hitched another ride. Weird, but normal for my brothers.

From the beginning, I was against any involvement, yet Pastor Keith knew something more. He had promises to fill.

In the process Aunt Kathy got recognized as the top Christian. Initially, I didn't think the Reverend needed me at all. He knew of her faith and commitment. Yes, Pastor Keith was a professional. He delivered countless memorials at Zion Gate Union. Yet, the fourth and final covenant was his dilemma. He knew Aunt Kathy and her array of evil. She wasn't a team player and wasn't fit for The Abyss. After all, Lucifer had standards and didn't need her challenges. So, by default, Heaven became the goal.

To me, Pastor Keith was a lot of things, but manipulator was never a thought. Meantime, he purposely pulled me in. He knew Saint Peter's and his requirements of forgiveness. Yep, Pastor Keith was a shrewd minister. He knew the Eulogy would transform and redeem me, too. Praises I dealt out could not be taken back. Wow, I never saw the set-up.

Moving on, my poem was complete and ready for delivery. Mind you, I was a renewed being. I'd promised to flush the hurt, hate, and all things bad. But shamefully, it read:

Ashes to Ashes
Dust to Dust
Death to Devil
You'll get Aunt Kathy first!

The verses were useless and obsolete, so I stayed mum and destroyed the rhyme.

The burial continued. They lowered Aunt Kathy's body into the soggy earth as Jerry and Tommy looked on. Still, I was ready. If I knew anything, I knew more stunts were in my brothers' trick bags.

Still, they stood together but on the opposite side of the grave. Then it happened! Jerry took off his leather jacket and out popped his secret bottle of whiskey. Ha! I was still good. On the other hand, the crowd was not. Rustling noises and snickers came from the audience. Jerry bent down and gradually recovered his hooch while wiping away the soft Mississippi mud. He thought nothing of his humiliation. As a matter of fact, he went further. "I got plenty of oil and a little some some if y'all need it." Fortunately, no one took the offer. However, he got more laughs and disgusting sighs to join the summer wind.

Shamefully, the crowd stared my way. Yet I held firm. To me, it could have been much worse, but it wasn't. I remained solid and stiff like the Statue of Liberty. Embarrassing, yes; but I was still ahead of the game.

Unfortunately, Jerry wasn't finished. He took off his shirt, tossed it in the hole, and then walked off the site. The crowd gasped again but with unspoken words and unpleasant looks of disdain! OK, he succeeded that time. But I stood motionless anyway. He got the same response our schizophrenic mom received during her episodes and outbursts. In other words, he still couldn't rattle me!

Up until then Tommy had been completely quiet, stationary, and somewhat dismissive. Noticeably, he wasn't wearing a coat at all. Being the goose to the gander, Tommy joined in the fray. He did likewise and took off his shirt. However, his fingers got caught in the webbing. Those rat holes just wouldn't let go. As much as he tried, he couldn't rid himself of that garment. It stuck to his fingers like a flag of surrender. By accident, Tommy had stolen the moment followed by bigger laughs and supporting cheers from the remaining mourners. It was refreshing and more acceptable than Jerry's opening antic. But eventually, Tommy got control and dropped his polo in the vault as well.

No one expected anything of that magnitude. Especially me! I'd seen some shit in my days, but this was icing and the cake. Meantime, the atmosphere suddenly changed from creepy and solemn to an edge of expectations. Everyone, including me, held their collective breath. Up until then, I was dignified, and a model in my neatly pressed Armani suit. I'd kept most of my emotions inside my skin. I was all about the business of the Memorial, the burial, and goodbye Mississippi.

Yet so much had gone off the rails. All eyes had turned to my brothers and me and not the grave. Even the crowd broke into splinter groups. For whatever reason, Pastor Keith never said a thing. He left me exposed to all my critics. Still, I hated being judged for the deeds of my brothers. But, if that was how it had to then so be it.

Then amazingly, something hit me right out of the blue! I wasn't completely whole nor totally cleansed. I kept Jerry and Tommy at a distance for far too long. I needed to do better. I needed to do right by them.

To my dismay, I needed Pastor Keith in a bad way. As I approached, I thanked him for his service and invitation. After all, he endured Aunt Kathy throughout the years. He gave her something beyond our derangements. Mom, Jerry, Tommy, and me were more than a notion. Lord knows, Aunt Kathy needed Pastor Keith and a Prayer-Line.

Then suddenly, everything came to a stop. It was half-time at a gravesite. That had to be a first. Yes, Aunt Kathy destroyed the lives of Mom, my brothers, and countless others; however, she was spiritually driven. Unfortunately, Satan had the wheel for most of her years.

But Pastor Keith did a solid better known a favor. He got Aunt Kathy a hook-up at the Pearly Gates. He went further and removed the venom from my heart.

So, I thanked him for his sermon. In return, he smiled and winked at me. "Reverend Hal, today, we made a great team. We were indeed a Two-Some! I must thank you as well. But Saint Peter is waiting." Wow sir, wow! I couldn't believe my ears. The Minister of Mississippi recognized me as a preacher! Yes, I was overjoyed and baffled, too. During the ceremony, Pastor Keith had sloshed around in the muck and mud like everyone else, yet he appeared unscathed. It just wasn't possible! There wasn't a spec nor a smidgen of dust anywhere on his person! Regardless, he was the man and deserved no explanations. I had no other logic and accepted him as such.

Obviously, my time was up, and it showed. "Sir, I'm out of here. May God continue to bless you and the members of Zion Gate Union Baptist Church!" Through all the lunacy, I failed to appreciate how neat and supportive my sweetheart had been. She remained unnerved, and as elegant as ever while proudly wearing the Catholic cross around her neck. However, I was deeply distracted and unable to address Deya's false beliefs. So, I gave her my blazer, took off my shirt, and placed it neatly across the tomb.

Meantime, Jerry and Tommy kept walking out of the churchyard. "Hey guys, wait up!" Immediately, I ran bare-chested out of the cemetery just like my brothers. It was time! It was time to build new bridges. According to Proverbs, "Pride comes before the Fall." I'd spent a lifetime climbing ladders and falling flat, all at the same time. Being stubborn and self-righteous didn't allow me to live.

Personally, "I thanked God, Pastor Keith, and Aunt Kathy for bringing my brothers and me back together. Sometimes death finds love in unknown places. Jerry, Tommy, and me renewed our brotherhood at a funeral. It was the biggest and best gift of them all. Yes, Aunt Kathy got her wings. Going forward, I plan to see her on the other side!

THE END

AFTERWORD

Thanks for reading *"My Bully, My Aunt, and Her Final Gift."* I hope you enjoyed this novel. If you are still curious about my writing style or wacky upbringing, you can find other books by me online as well. Such as "Surviving Chaos: How I Found Peace at A Beach Bar."

Stay updated to events and new releases by joining my mailing list/club of readers at **hephifer@yahoo.com**.

Like me on Facebook: HaroldPhifer2024

Follow me on X (Twitter): @hephifer

Do take a moment and drop a review(s) with your selective site(s). No doubt, your opinion will inspire others to share their experiences and do likewise. Please know your feedback is greatly appreciated.

Finally, visit my website: RiseAndRead.com. You will see other books that reflect my visions and spirit of writing.

Thank you again, dear reader! I hope we continue to meet and share a few laughs between the pages.

With God's love,

Harold Phifer